Keep on reading Savannah!

What in Carnation

Isabella Proctor Cozy Mysteries
Book 2

Lisa Bouchard

Lisa B

For Paul, who supports all my crazy dreams.

Table of Contents

Chapter 1

Running a business wasn't easy.

It had been three months since I inherited the Portsmouth Apothecary from my mentor and friend Trina Bassett. She was murdered by a man who kidnapped the object of his obsession—my best friend, Abby—and was angry at Trina for not making him a love potion.

I ran my hands along the smooth cherry desktop in the office. I'd been working on my laptop for over an hour; there were about a hundred tabs open on my browser and pages of handwritten notes next to the keyboard.

I sat back and threw my pencil on the desk, frustrated about how something that seemed so simple could be so difficult. Birds chirped outside and called my attention out the window to the greenhouse in the courtyard behind the shop. Late spring sun shone on the glass, and one of the ventilation panels on the roof opened. It would be warm inside, and I longed to go walk down the two aisles of plants and breathe in the floral-scented air. Unfortunately, I couldn't.

Responsibility called, and I needed to choose new suppliers. Every company had different pricing, different shipping costs, and different billing cycles. I was beginning to think I'd need a few college courses, if not a whole degree, to make sure I didn't run this business into the ground.

I needed a break. I grabbed my green "I'm an herbalist, what's your superpower?" mug and walked out to the complimentary tea station for more caffeine.

I'd instituted having caffeinated and decaf teas available for customers; today's tea was mango matcha. I poured more of the caffeinated in my mug and stirred in a dollop of honey. Goddess give me strength to deal with learning almost everything on the job.

I loved my customers, and they made all this work worth it. Mrs. Newcomb's raspy cough seemed to be clearing up with her new potion, and lately I'd noticed an uptick in first-time customers. Hopefully, in a week or two, many of them would return to be second-time and then long-term customers.

The door chimes rang, and Agatha walked in. Agatha was the only client I felt like I'd failed. Her brown hair was matted, and she was wearing mismatched shoes. Her blouse was half-tucked into loose jeans that hung low on her hips, telling me she hadn't been eating enough. The voice in her head, Alice, must have been strong. "Good morning, Agatha. How are you?" I asked.

She walked straight to the tea station and poured herself a mug of decaf. "Horrible."

I said nothing. I knew she'd continue as long as I didn't interrupt.

"Alice is angry because I keep trying to shut her up, and sometimes she won't let me take my medicine. She makes me dump it out instead." She looked from her mug to me, tears welling in her eyes. "I try not to. She's stronger than me, and when she doesn't let me sleep, I can't stop her."

I put my hand on her shoulder. "Oh, Agatha, how terrible."

She took a sip of her tea. "I don't know what to do, and I want to give up. Just let her control the body so I can sleep and not fight for *every single thing* I want in life."

My heart broke for her. I hadn't been able to find a potion that did more than keep some of her symptoms at bay. Honestly, treating mental illness was far outside my abilities, but she refused to get help anywhere else.

"Do you think it's time to go see my friend, Dr. Rebecca?" I held my hands up to forestall her objections. "I know you don't want to. I feel helpless, though, and there's nothing more I can do for you."

Rebecca Cleary was a local psychiatrist I'd called when I realized my potions couldn't cure Agatha. She wasn't happy about Agatha relying on potions and wanted me to bring her in for a consultation. I didn't want to nag Agatha, because as far as I knew, I was the only person watching her health. If she stopped coming to see me, I wasn't sure she'd have anyone in her life who cared about her.

"Alice won't let me."

"Please. I'll come with you and make sure nothing bad happens. All we have to do is talk to the doctor for a little bit. You don't need to take any other medicine, just talk."

Agatha shook her head and banged her mug down on the tea table. "I need my meds, then I have to go."

I sighed. "Okay. Take the first dose here, where I can see you." I'd instituted this rule with her a month ago, hoping it would get her back on the path to taking regular doses. Given the way she looked today, my plan didn't seem to be working. Before I gave her the bottle, I closed my eyes and used my intuition to make sure the potion I'd made for her was still the right one. All I saw was ashwagandha, which was what was waiting for her behind the counter.

My intuition guided me to make the appropriate potions for people. I closed my eyes and thought about the person, then I would see what they needed. I'd made one potion for my grandma without having her with me, and she'd had hallucinations because the formulation wasn't correct for her. Now I always made sure to check my work with the person in the room.

She rubbed her hands on her pants. "Fine. Whatever."

"Great. It's waiting for you at the register."

We walked to the back of the shop, and I pulled her bottle out from under the counter. I twisted the lid off and held the bottle out to her with a plastic spoon. "Two spoonfuls."

She frowned as she accepted the spoon and bottle. She poured one spoonful and took it, then the second. "There. Are you happy now?"

I smiled encouragingly. "I am. I worry about you. I'm afraid someday Alice is going to hurt you."

She took the cap from my hand and screwed it onto her bottle. "So am I," she whispered before she fled the building.

I rested my head in my hands, wishing I could do something else for her. I'd already talked to Grandma and the aunts, the people I relied on most for advice. Even though they were more experienced witches than me, they didn't have nearly as much potion knowledge and had no other suggestions.

The nearest potion witch I knew of was Hester Johnson in Sewall, but I hadn't had time to visit her yet. I needed to make that a priority. If I could get Agatha to come with me, Hester might even be able to find a cure for her.

I looked out the picture window at the people walking by and was surprised to see Caroline Arneson staring through the window at me. She had been standing outside the apothecary intermittently for the last two months, staring in. I didn't know why; maybe she was trying to intimidate me?

Agatha hadn't paid me. In fact, she hadn't paid me for weeks. I took ten dollars out of my pocket and rang up the transaction. My accountant would pitch a fit if he knew I was doing this, so we'll keep this our little secret.

No sooner had Agatha left than my mother walked in. She was dressed for work at Bayfield Nursery, in jeans and a T-shirt, rather than her usual flowing dress.

"Hi, Mom, what's up?" There had to be something up for her to stop by before work.

She grinned at me. "I have found the perfect guy for you. My boss's son has come home from college. His father is worried about him and said he needed a few new friends."

I rolled my eyes. "New friends, or a girlfriend?"

She shifted her weight from side to side. "I thought the two of you could go on a date, and if that didn't work out, you could be friends."

"You realize relationships usually work the other way around, right?"

She blew a strand of hair out of her face. "I let it slip at work that you were single, and Mr. Bayfield thinks you and Geoffrey would make a great couple."

"How would he know?"

She bit her lip. "I may have talked you up a little. You and your cousins really have to start thinking about settling down."

I glared at her.

"What? You can't blame me for being proud of you and how well you've handled the curve balls you've had lately."

She knew I was glaring about settling down, but I let it slide. There had never been a doubt in my mind that my mother loved me, but hearing she was proud of me made me smile. "Thanks."

"Can I give him your number?" she asked.

"Okay. One date is all I'll commit to. If it doesn't work out, it ends there."

"Understood. I'm sure he'll call soon."

As my mother walked to the door, Caroline Arneson held it open for her. Caroline's overly-processed blonde hair had been teased and pulled back into a loose bun, giving her a messier look than I was used to seeing. She was also wearing flats. Was she trying out a more casual style, maybe relaxing a bit? There was no sense in assuming she was here to bully me into selling my shop. After all, she had promised to stop. "Good morning. How can I help you today?"

She lowered her sunglasses to reveal a black eye. Well, I say "black," but the color was more yellow-green, meaning the bruise was a few days old and healing up. When I questioned her about Trina's death, Caroline confided that she knew how to handle her husband's anger. It didn't seem like she succeeded recently.

"Are you okay?" I asked.

"Of course I am. I just need something to speed up the healing."

I frowned. I'd been gathering resources for abused women for months now; if Caroline ever needed them, I hoped I'd have an opportunity to give them to her. "I can help. Can we talk in my office first?"

She smiled. "Are you ready to close this failing business so I can buy your space?"

She looked me up and down and frowned, as though I didn't pass muster. "You need a few thousand dollars to revamp your wardrobe. I could help."

"I'm not closing, and the business is doing fine, thank you. I have something for you in my desk."

She followed me into my office and sat. I opened one of my desk drawers and pulled out a folder. "I worry about you, since you told me about your husband." I handed her the folder.

She opened the folder and scoffed. "This isn't for me. I can handle him."

She tossed the folder onto my desk.

"Are you sure? Your eye seems to tell a different story."

She stood up. "You're just a kid, what do you know? Now, can you sell me anything or not?"

"Yes. I've got a nice mixture of aloe, arnica, and bromelain that should do the trick. It's out in the shop."

I followed her out of the office.

"Seems like you've bounced back from the robbery. It looks good in here," she said.

I handed her a small jar of a bruise-fading ointment. "Thanks. I've put in a lot of work, but I think I'm doing well."

She inspected the floors, which I'd washed the previous night. "I won't even need to hire a cleaning crew when I move in here. How much do I owe you?"

I blew my breath out. "Nothing, if you stop asking me to leave the building."

Her lips quirked into a small smile. "Guess I'd better pay you, then."

I held out my hand. "Eleven dollars."

As she fished through her bag for money, I stared at her, allowing my intuition to see if she needed anything else. Of course! The ingredients for Harmony

Wash filled my vision: red rose petals, African violets, clover, crocus, elecampane, lemon verbena, and cinnamon. "I have something else for you."

"For the bruise?"

"No. I've got a great floral bubble bath. You look like a relaxing bath would do you good." I wasn't really lying to her. It was a floral bubble bath, but if I told her using it would bring harmony to her home, she'd laugh at me and probably not take it. "It's right over here."

I led her to the display of bubble baths I'd created over the last month. "It's a new line of product I've created."

I held out a bottle to her. "On the house."

She handed me eleven dollars and took the bubble bath from my hands. "Thanks, kid."

I was about to go back to my computer and the hundred open tabs when my neighbor Mrs. Thompson walked into the store. Without her, we might never have caught Chuck, the man who killed Trina and kidnapped Abby. Since that horrible week this past March, Mrs. Thompson and I had been having tea together a couple times a week. She invited me over at what seemed to be the most random times for a chat. She was a witch, too, although she never told me much about herself. All I knew was that she could track and find people with her magic. She wanted to know about me, my plans, and what I saw myself doing in the future. Some days it seemed like I was in a months-long interview for an unnamed job.

My future seemed set in stone to me: run the apothecary, learn as much as I could about potion making, and help people whenever possible.

She never seemed satisfied with my answer, but didn't hint about what else she wanted to hear. She also played a mean game of cribbage, and more than once, I wondered if her cards were marked, or if she used magic to win. The number of twenty-four-point hands she got was ridiculous.

Today she was dressed in seersucker Capri pants, boat shoes, and a blue polo shirt. She looked like any other gray-haired grandmother out shopping. I knew better. She had a sharp mind and a dry sense of humor.

"Hey, Mrs. T., how are you?" I asked as she approached the counter.

"Just fine, Miss P."

She'd asked me to call her Beatrice, but I didn't feel right about using her first name. She was my elder, and Grandma had made sure we all respected our elders, particularly those who were witches. In retaliation, Mrs. Thompson called me Miss P., rather than Isabella. It was a good compromise.

I searched the shelf of prepared potions under the counter and didn't see any for her. "Are you here to pick something up?" I asked.

"Oh, no, dear. Jameson is doing fine. Whatever you've done to change his tonic has worked wonders."

Jameson was her black cat. I know, I know, what a stereotype. Then again, black cats needed good homes too. Jameson had kidney problems, and Trina had developed a tonic for him. I made the same potion, and mine seemed to be working better for him.

"What can I do for you?" I asked.

Sadness crossed her face for a moment, before it vanished. "I have to go on a trip sometime soon, and I wanted to ask you to watch Jameson."

"Of course." He and I got along well, and he didn't even mind moving over to my apartment the other times I'd taken care of him. "Going anyplace fun?"

"Not this time, I'm afraid. I've got family business to deal with, and it can't be sorted out over the phone."

"No problem. Just say the word, and I'll be there. How long will you be gone?"

She sighed. "Several days, so make sure you take the food and kitty litter with you."

She grabbed my hand and squeezed. "There's no one I trust more with Jameson than you."

I smiled. "That's kind of you to say. I think he likes me, too."

She let go of my hand and forced a weak smile. "Good. I'm glad the two of you get along well."

I wanted to ask why she looked sad. "Stay for some tea. I've made mango matcha, but I can make anything else you want."

"No, thank you, dear. I've got other errands to run before I leave town. And when I get back, you and I need to have a long talk."

I had no idea what she meant by that. "Sure. About what?"

She frowned. "Your future."

11

It was never good when someone frowned when they mentioned your future. She walked out into the sunshine, and a sense of dread washed over me. This trip would not be good for her.

Chapter 2

My cell phone rang, and I looked at the screen before I answered. I didn't recognize the number. "Hello?"

"Hi, is this Izzy Proctor?"

Clearly not a person who knew me. "This is Isabella."

"Oh, good. Hi. This is Geoff Bayfield. My dad said I should call you."

"Right, hi. My mother told me you'd call."

"Great! I was thinking we could go out for dinner. How about tonight?"

I paused for a minute, pretending I was checking my calendar. Did I really want to do this? I mean, how pathetic was it to be set up by your mother? Probably about as bad as being set up by your father. Not nearly as embarrassing as having absolutely nothing on my social calendar though.

"Sure, I'm free. How about seven, at The Rosa?"

"Sounds good. I'll see you then."

I stood in the entry of The Rosa Restaurant. No one was waiting for me, so I surveyed the tables in the dining room. No single men there either.

For what seemed like the millionth time, I wondered how I let my mother talk me into this date.

"Table for one, miss?" a host asked.

I turned to face his wedding ring and smirk of superiority. Here was a man who wouldn't ever have to eat alone if he didn't want to. And wasn't that one of my mother's selling points for dating and marriage? Not that settling down with someone had done her, or my aunts, any good.

Aunt Lily had never married Thea's father, and whatever happened between them was bad enough that we never spoke of him.

Aunt Nadia's husband had crept out of Proctor House in the middle of the night, leaving a note and a hundred dollars, as if either were sufficient compensation for abandoning his family.

My parents had divorced when I was three, and I had no memory of my dad—only photos. For most of my life, that was fine. Grandpa was an excellent substitute for our missing fathers during soccer games, father-daughter dances, and when we needed someone to understand when we thought our mothers were being unreasonable.

We were lucky to have him as long as we did, but I still missed him during times like this. I could hear him in my mind, chastising my mother. "Michelle, leave the child alone. Getting married young didn't do you a lick of good, did it? Let her find her own way in life."

"Miss?"

"I'm waiting for someone. Is there a bar?" I asked.

He frowned, probably impatient at having to watch me think. "Through the dining room and to the left."

"Thanks."

I walked through the dimly lit dining room, tables groaning with all the carbs a person could want—focaccia with herbed dipping oil, lasagna, pizza with any topping imaginable, and a delicious-looking fettucine primavera.

My stomach growled, and I hoped my date was there. The sooner we ate, the happier my stomach would be and the happier I'd be to never have to see him again. I supposed I ought to have given him the benefit of the doubt, but I just couldn't.

My mother worked in a garden center, mostly for fun, and Geoff was the owner's son. He was twenty-four, had returned home from college, and was looking to settle down in the Portsmouth area.

How many red flags could one guy wave? Did he really take two extra years to finish college? Couldn't he find a job that his parents didn't give him, and didn't

15

he want to see the world, instead of staying close to home?

I was substantially underwhelmed.

To be fair, how did I look in a quick three-sentence description? I didn't even go to college, I came from the "weird" family in town, and I had a tendency to find dead bodies.

Yeah, I wasn't sure I'd date me either.

I took a seat at the bar and ordered a seltzer with lime.

"Starting a tab?" the bartender asked.

"Yes. I'm meeting someone for dinner."

The clock behind the bar said it was seven, so in one more minute, he'd officially be late. Was there an appropriate amount of time to wait for a date? Could I leave after five minutes? Ten?

I looked past the bartender and into the mirror behind him. A tall blond man with a linebacker's shoulders walked into the bar, looked around, and made a beeline to me.

"Excuse me, are you Isabella?" he asked.

I turned to face him. A smile crept onto my traitorous lips. I didn't want to enjoy the date, but goddess, was he easy on the eyes. "Yes. Geoffrey?"

He returned my smile. "Do you want to eat here, or would you like a table?"

"Definitely a table," I said.

Once the surprised host seated us, we started in with the awkward, first-date questions. I'd pay good money for a way to skip right to the fifth date, where you already knew each other and didn't have to endure this stilted small talk.

16

"Your mother tried to explain what you do for work. I didn't really understand. You're a barista, right, only with tea instead of coffee?"

I couldn't imagine any way my mother would describe making potions to sound like a barista.

"Not really. I make herbal remedies—balms, tinctures, and teas—to heal people, relieve their stress, and help them enjoy life more."

"You're a doctor? That's not at all what she said."

"No. I'm definitely not a doctor. My title is herbalist, and I spent a year as an apprentice before I started working on my own. I use plants to help heal people."

"You only spent a year in college? Totally unfair. My dad made me spend four—okay, five and a half—for a business degree, and I'm still stuck in the warehouse driving a forklift."

I smiled to disguise my dismay at his intellectual wattage. My mother definitely didn't warn me that he sounded like a stereotypical business major. One more try. "I make things like tea, from plants, for people."

His face lit up. Maybe something had sparked in his brain.

"Oh, like weed! I get it, you work in a dispensary. That's cool. Do you work in Maine or Massachusetts? Or do you work in an illegal New Hampshire one?"

I sighed. "None." I pulled out one of the twenty business cards I'd had printed and handed it to him. I wasn't sure he was the best use of my limited card stash, but I couldn't explain my job any differently. "You should come visit; you'll get a better idea of what I do if you see the apothecary."

He put the card in his wallet. "Cool. My new girlfriend has business cards."

I opened my menu to cover my eye roll. He opened his, and we spent a few blissful minutes not talking.

I set my menu down. "I'll have the pasta primavera. I saw someone in the bar with it, and it looked delicious."

He frowned. "I can't eat that many carbs. They'll kill you, y'know. I'm having the antipasto and meatballs."

I like appetizers as much as the next person, but I also liked a real meal. "Anything else?"

He frowned. "Too many carbs. I like to save them for the weekend."

Who was I to complain about his dietary restrictions? They were clearly working for him.

He set his menu down. "You're into natural living, right?"

Was I? Probably not as much as you'd expect from an herbalist. I liked a good can of store-bought soup, and life wouldn't be worth living without hot dogs cooked over a fire at least once in the summer.

"Sort of. I guess it's a process. What do you eat for your weekend carbs?"

He grinned. "I save them all for beer."

"That's a lot of beer, isn't it?"

He leaned forward. This was clearly a topic he loved to talk about. "Not as much as you might think. I don't eat carbs during the week. Tonight is special because we're here. The antipasto platter has vegetables, so I budget about 16 grams of carbs in my food, leaving me enough left over at the end of the week for about thirty-five light beers."

My eyes widened. Thirty-five? One short of six six-packs? I wished we were in a brighter restaurant, because I had the urge to check his eyes for a yellow color indicating alcoholic hepatitis.

"That seems like a lot," I said.

"You get used to it."

Why? Why would anyone want to get used to so much beer?

"What else do you do on weekends?"

"My weekends are sweet! I leave work at noon on Friday, pick up the beer and head to a buddy's house. Me and the guys spend the weekend there, watching sports, drinking beer, hanging out."

My mind couldn't help doing the math. Thirty-five cans of beer in 60 hours. Not too bad, if he didn't sleep, maybe?

Before I could come up with a comment, our waiter came. "Are you ready to order?"

I handed him my menu. "I'd like the pasta primavera, please."

Geoff set his menu on the table. "Antipasto and meatballs, as a meal."

"Very good. Anything to drink?"

I had planned to have a glass of wine, but was suddenly conscious of all the carbs in my dinner. "Seltzer with lime, please."

The waiter looked at Geoff, who finally said, "Better save the carbs for the weekend. Just water."

Our waiter left, and I decided to turn the conversation to something we had in common. "I inherited my business a few months ago, and running it is a lot more difficult than I anticipated. A business degree might be useful, although it's tough to squeeze in classes when you're the only person running the shop as well."

Geoff nodded.

"What do you think?" I prompted him.

"When I finally inherit the nursery, I'm going to relax. My dad does a lot of the work himself. I'm going to hire people to do all the hard stuff, so I can chill out and rake in the money."

"Do you have any siblings that can help you?"

He grinned. "Nope. I'm an only child. It's great not to worry about splitting up the inheritance."

"Does the business make enough that you can hire more people?" I asked.

He looked at me like he hadn't considered that. "I don't know. I guess if it doesn't, I'll sell more stuff. As for going to business school, I guess it might help. I didn't actually learn too much. Like the guys in my fraternity said, it's all about the connections, and as long as the GPA winds up at 2.0, they can't refuse you your diploma."

I looked around the restaurant, hoping to see a friend, an enemy, a fire in the kitchen, anything that could get me out of this date. Why hadn't I set up an emergency call with Delia?

"You know, if you're having problems with your business, I can come by and give you some advice."

I turned my attention back to Geoff. "That's thoughtful of you. You sound busy at your own job, that forklift isn't going to drive itself, and I don't want to take you away from it."

He smiled. "Nah. I'm the boss's son. If I want to take an afternoon off, no one will rat me out. They wouldn't dare."

Geoff changed the topic abruptly. "So how about you? Do you have any siblings?"

"Yes, and no."

"Doesn't it have to be one or the other?" he asked.

"I had a twin who died as a baby."

"Way to bring the room down," Geoff said.

Wow. I already had low expectations for this date, but I guess maybe a little empathy would have been nice. "I also have two cousins who are my age, and we were all raised together. They feel like I imagine having sisters would be like."

Mercifully, our orders were delivered before we could delve further into my family history.

My pasta looked delicious. I closed my eyes and inhaled the aroma. When I opened my eyes, Geoff was already eating his meatballs.

At least he wasn't talking with his mouth full.

We ate in silence for about fifteen minutes. He finished before I did and watched me eat my last few bites.

When I finished, he shook his head. "So many carbs."

I set my napkin on the table. "Well, Geoff, this has been a lovely dinner, but I need to call it a night."

"Oh," he said. "I thought we could go for a walk after dinner and talk more."

I didn't think he wanted to walk, or talk. I was getting more of a make-out-in-an-alley vibe from him. "I can't. I've got a busy morning and need to get home."

"At least let me drive you," he offered.

"That's not necessary. I've got paperwork to catch up on in my office. It's only a couple blocks from here, and I'd like to walk."

I stood up and walked toward the exit. After a moment he followed after me. I made it out the door before he caught up to me.

I walked toward the apothecary, which was also the way home. I had no plans to stop at work, but there was no way I wanted him to know where I lived.

"Kiss goodnight?" he asked my retreating back.

I pretended I didn't hear him and kept walking.

Chapter 3

When I first inherited the apothecary, I considered expanding the morning hours. I'm glad I didn't. Opening at ten allowed me to occasionally sleep in, run a few errands, or like today, tidy up my apartment and take out the trash.

As I walked down the hall, white trash bag in hand, Jameson's loud wails were unmistakable. I knocked on Mrs. Thompson's door, but there was no answer.

"Mrs. T.?" I called.

Jameson scratched at the door and howled louder. A chill ran through me. I'd only felt this chill when someone was dead.

I unlocked the door and slowly opened it. "Mrs. T.?" I called again.

Jameson howled and ran out of the apartment. I turned and watched as he stopped at my door. "Good. Stay there," I told him.

I left the door open and stepped inside her apartment. I scanned the living and dining area. Her lace-covered dining table was cleared off, and the chairs were pushed in. A maroon-and-cream afghan was folded and draped neatly over her couch. In the kitchen, dry dishes waited in her dish drainer to be put away. Everything looked normal and very tidy. I set my bag of trash down and called to her. "Mrs. Thompson? It's Isabella."

There was no answer in the silent apartment.

I peeked into her bathroom, which was the mirror image of mine. Everything was tidy, and the sink and bathtub were dry.

She had turned one of the bedrooms into a study. The only bit of disarray in the room was on her opened rolltop desk. Papers were strewn across it, and a pen rested on a half-written letter addressed to Rosemarie.

Only one room left to look in: her bedroom. The door was closed, and I knocked on it. I didn't know why I expected an answer. My heart raced with fear for Mrs. T. I slowly reached for her door handle, afraid of what I might find. I pushed open the door and saw nothing in the dark room. I flipped the wall switch, and her bedside light turned on.

Heavy velvet curtains blocked the morning sun and gave the room an ominous feel. Mrs. Thompson was laying in her bed, blankets pulled up. She was on her back with her arms on top of the blankets, across her chest. Her gray hair was tucked behind her ears. Her chest wasn't rising and falling with breath.

"Mrs. T.," I said gently. She didn't move. I walked to the side of the bed and put my hand on her exposed wrist. Her cold skin told me not to bother looking for a pulse.

I pulled my hand back and stepped away from the bed.

Three months ago, I found my mentor bludgeoned to death outside the apothecary. That horrible scene still fueled my nightmares. Mrs. T., on the other hand, looked like she had fallen asleep and never woke up.

I backtracked out of the bedroom, turning the light off as I headed out of the apartment. I locked her door and rushed to mine, where Jameson was waiting.

"Come on in, sweetie," I said as I opened my door. "It's not good, you know. She's gone."

Jameson meowed and rubbed against my leg. I bent down to scratch him between the ears.

In the kitchen, I filled a bowl with water and set it down for him. "I'll have to get your food later on."

He ignored the water, jumped up on the couch, and stretched before lying down. I pulled my phone out of my pocket and dialed Detective Steve Palmer.

I hadn't seen him since he took my statement after we found Abby in the trunk of Chuck's car, but I wanted to speak to someone I knew, not some nameless 911 operator.

"Isabella? Are you okay?" he asked.

"Yes . . . uh, I'm fine. Mrs. Thompson, my neighbor, she's dead."

"And how do you know this?" he asked. "Never mind. Where is she?"

"In her apartment. I'm in mine."

"Good, stay there. I'll be there in ten minutes."

I sat on my couch next to Jameson and dialed my cousin Thea.

"Isabella? What's up?" she mumbled groggily.

"Were you still sleeping? I can call back later," I said.

"Too late now, I'm awake."

"Okay. I'm sorry to start your day off with bad news—"

Thea interrupted me. "Are you okay? Where are you? Delia and I can be there right away."

It was nice to know my cousins were ready to rescue me at the drop of a hat, but maybe I should call them more often when I didn't have bad news, so they didn't jump to conclusions.

"I'm fine. I'm in my apartment. It's Mrs. Thompson, she passed in her sleep."

I reached out to pet Jameson. He needed the comfort as much as I did.

"Oh no. I'm so sorry. I can still come over."

"No, don't. Detective Palmer will be here soon and he's going to have a million questions to ask me. Maybe I'll see you tonight."

"Absolutely. We can come over whenever you want."

"Don't tell the aunts yet. Let me talk to them after the police have left."

Thea chuckled. "You couldn't pay me enough to tell them."

The aunts, our collective term for my mother, Thea's mother, and Delia's mother, would pitch a fit when they heard I'd found another dead woman. After nine months, they still hadn't given up on browbeating me to move back to Proctor House, and this would refuel their drive.

"I'm going to wait until Palmer can officially tell me she died in her sleep."

"Smart." Thea yawned. "Call me later on."

When I hung up the phone, Jameson started running in the apartment. Back and forth, from me to the door.

"What is it?" I asked him, feeling a little silly because it wasn't like he was going to answer me.

I tried to extend my senses to him, but I couldn't read anything from a cat. He was getting agitated, and I was afraid he was going to hurt himself.

"Come here, Jameson."

He ran to me, and I scooped him up. When he realized I was walking to my bedroom and not the apartment door, he howled and scratched my arm.

"Ow! Cut it out," I said as I put him in my room and quickly closed the door.

Chapter 4

I settled into the couch and waited for Palmer to come. I didn't know what else to do. No, wait, that wasn't true.

I knew exactly what to do when I found a dead woman. Call the police and wait for the inevitable questioning. The real question was how many dead people would I find in my lifetime? Once is happenstance, twice is coincidence, three times is enemy action—at least according to James Bond.

What enemy? All I wanted to do was make potions, help people feel better, and live a quiet, magical life under the radar. It made a gruesome kind of sense that Chuck had overreacted and killed Trina, or that James had me drugged so he could force me to give him the apothecary. I couldn't understand why someone would want to murder Mrs. Thompson. As far as I knew, she led a quiet life in retirement. She certainly didn't act like a woman with enemies.

Jameson finally stopped howling in my room. I hoped he found a nice patch of sun and decided to nap.

If Mrs. T. had enemies, wouldn't she at least move around more often? Then again, I hadn't known her long; perhaps she was about to leave town.

I heard a small meow that didn't seem to come from behind my bedroom door. Had the cat gotten out of my room?

I got up and looked down the hallway. Jameson was there, looking calm and even a little sheepish about having scratched me. "I'm going to pick you up again, and you're going to be nice, right?"

I picked him up, and he didn't scratch me. This was good. I went back to the couch and sat. "What was all that about?"

We stayed there for a few minutes. He seemed fine, although I was still worried he'd freak out on me again.

I set Jameson down on the couch. I needed to make coffee before the police came. In the kitchen, I took the bag of pricey Kona beans my mother had given me for my birthday and ground enough for a pot. I hoped the police appreciated I was using my stash of good coffee for them. As the water dripped through the beans, I inhaled the strong aroma and decided too much caffeine would keep me jittery all day. I needed a calming, herbal tea to help me deal with the stress the day promised.

Jameson hopped off the couch and drank some water. He looked up at me, and I knew he wanted food. "I know, boy. I promise I'll get some soon. Right now we've got to wait until the police show up."

I scooped him up and rubbed my nose in his fur. "It's too bad you can't talk. You could tell me what happened, and the police could close the case immediately."

He patted my face with his paw and blurted a meow at me. I felt comforted by his touch, like we had an emotional connection. That couldn't be. He was just a cat.

"I don't know if you have anywhere else to go either. I'll check with Mrs. Thompson's family. You can always stay with me if they don't want to take you."

I was rewarded with another blurt and he bumped my chin with his forehead. So far, so good. He'd always been affectionate with me, and losing his owner hadn't seemed to change that.

"I take it you want to stay? I'm sure Abby won't mind."

I put Jameson down to make myself tea. Was there a potion to make cats talk? None that I recalled from reading the potion books in my office. Since I took over the apothecary, I'd devoted an hour a day to reading the spell books Trina had acquired. Reading them was a double-edged sword. On one hand, I was learning more than I thought possible. On the other, I often ended my reading sessions worried that I hardly knew anything about the business I was running.

It was tough going it alone.

I wasn't actually alone, though. I had my family. My family who didn't have more than average talent with potion making. They were great for moral support, but practical questions like "Do I slice the root horizontally or vertically?" were out of their league. And mine, too.

I poured the now-boiling water into my favorite forest-green mug.

I was going to miss Mrs. Thompson.

Over cribbage and tea, we talked about life. My life mostly. She deflected almost all questions about herself. I knew she had a son named Brent, but she never mentioned a husband, siblings, or even her parents. I had the impression she and Brent didn't get along well, and even though I had urged her to seek reconciliation, she said it would never work.

I felt sorry for her, living alone with no relatives she wanted to see. I couldn't imagine how lonely she must have been. Maybe that's why she had Jameson, to keep her company. I'd have to write Brent a condolence letter, telling him about my friendship with Mrs. T. so he would know she hadn't been alone. I hoped he'd find comfort in that.

I took my tea to the couch and sat. Yesterday, she said she wanted to talk about my future. What about my future? My future at the apothecary? My future as a witch? Something else? I should have asked her to clarify before she left. At least then I'd have an idea of what she meant.

I wondered if she had something written down in her apartment. After Palmer left, I'd have to go in and take a look around. I wouldn't touch anything— okay, I wouldn't touch anything without gloves—and I'd leave everything where I found it. He'd never know I was there. Besides, I had to get cat supplies for Jameson.

Chapter 5

A loud knock at my door startled me and sent Jameson running to my room. It wasn't like him to be spooked that easily. I looked through the peephole, then let Palmer and Kate in.

I hadn't seen either of them in months. Kate looked more harried and had some serious bags under her eyes. Her uniform also looked more worn out—it wasn't the brand new, shiny uniform it had been when I first met her. Even her name tag had a scratch across the S in Stanton.

Palmer looked about the same, though he must have been spending more time outside, because he had a tan.

"Are you okay?" he asked.

I hesitated at the loaded question. Physically, I was fine. Emotionally, I wasn't doing so well. Most people never find a dead body, and now I'd found two in the span of less than three and a half months. "Yes, I'm fine."

He gave me a skeptical look but let my lie slide. "I'll come take your statement after I see the scene."

Kate avoided my eyes and didn't see the smile I tried to give her. I closed the door and went back to my couch. I felt like I couldn't do anything until they were done next door. Jameson poked his head out of my bedroom door, saw the coast was clear, and joined me on the couch.

After twenty minutes and lots more people going up and down the stairs, there was another knock at my door.

Jameson jumped off the couch and ran into my bedroom again. I opened the door, feeling safe with so many police next door. "Come on in. Can I get you coffee?" I asked them.

"No," Kate said snippily.

"No, thanks. I don't think this will take long," Palmer said, smoothing over Kate's rudeness.

I gestured to the couch. "Okay. Have a seat."

They sat, and I pulled one of the dining chairs over to sit in front of them.

"Start at the beginning, tell me everything," Palmer said.

"It all started when I heard Jameson yowling when I took the trash out this morning."

"Who is Jameson?" Kate asked.

"Mrs. Thompson's cat. Anyway, I knocked a couple times, then let myself in. I looked in all the rooms and found her in bed. I touched her wrist, looking for a pulse. Her skin was so cold, I knew she was gone."

"That answers one question," Kate said.

"What?"

"Why a bag of your trash was in her living room."

Oh bats! I can't believe I completely forgot to take my trash out with me. "I'm sorry. I can throw it out now."

Kate shook her head. "It's part of the crime scene. We've got techs going through it for evidence."

Evidence? That hardly seemed necessary. "Really, it's just trash from my apartment I was going to take out this morning. My garbage has nothing to do with Mrs. Thompson."

"We'll throw it out when we're done," she said.

Palmer looked at Kate and she frowned. "What did you touch in the apartment?" he asked.

I thought for a moment, retracing my steps in my mind. "I opened the apartment door, opened her bedroom door, and turned her bedroom light on and off. Then I closed her bedroom and apartment doors."

"That's all?" Kate asked. "You didn't play amateur detective and rifle through her drawers looking for clues?"

"The other doors were open, and I only needed light in her bedroom." I paused for a moment. "I've been in her apartment many times over the past few months. You'll probably find my fingerprints everywhere."

Kate snorted, and Palmer gave her another look, this one more pointed.

"Why would I look for clues?" I asked. "She looked like she passed in her sleep."

"What else did you notice?" Palmer asked.

"Everything seemed tidy and neat, except her desk, and Jameson was upset and ran out of the apartment when I first opened the door."

Kate pulled out her notepad. "Did you see or hear anything last night or early this morning that seemed out of place?"

"No. Abby's bedroom shares a wall with hers. Maybe she did?"

"Where is she now?" Palmer asked.

"The Fancy Tart," I said.

"And Mrs. Thompson has been your neighbor for how long?" Kate asked.

"Abby and I have been here for about nine months, and she moved in about a month after we did."

Kate wrote a few things in her notepad. "Ever hear any arguments over there?"

I shook my head. "No. She was a quiet woman, went to the grocery store twice a week, stopped by the apothecary regularly for a tonic for Jameson."

"You treat cats?" Palmer asked.

"Not usually. Trina came up with this treatment for him."

I frowned at the thought of Trina. I missed her every day.

New voices sounded in the hallway. Palmer looked to Kate, who stood up and went to investigate, leaving the two of us alone.

I had been disappointed Palmer hadn't called me over the last few months. I thought, after a rocky beginning, that we had hit it off. I guess I was wrong. I considered calling him, asking him out for coffee, but I always ended up chickening out.

Palmer relaxed into the sofa. "I'm not happy you've found another dead woman."

I grimaced. "Same."

"Kate still hasn't forgiven you."

I sighed. "I know. I tried calling her, left apologies on her voicemail. She never returned my calls. It's too bad, because I hoped we could be friends. Are you sure I can't get you coffee?" I asked.

"Best not to risk it," he said.

Then I got it. I'd lost his trust too. I looked down at my hands. "I understand. I'm sorry." I looked up and decided I needed to explain my actions. "It's just that if we hadn't given Kate the tea, she never would have let us leave, and if we hadn't left, we might not have found Abby in time."

"We'll never know what might have happened." He sat forward, staring at me intensely. "Whatever happens here, I don't want you involved. Right now you're an innocent bystander. If you poke your nose in, you'll move to suspect so fast your head will spin." He glared at me. "Am I making myself clear?"

I bit my lip and nodded. If this was how he felt about me, it's a good thing he hadn't called.

Kate walked back in. "The landlord wanted to know what was going on. I sent him to his apartment and told him we'd be down to question him—"

She put her hand to her temple and rubbed.

"Are you okay?" I asked.

She shook her head. "Headache. It'll go away sooner or later."

I looked into her eyes, trying to figure out what she needed. Still feverfew. "You've really got to cut down on the stress in your life. Do you have any more of the feverfew I gave you? It should help."

Kate gently shook her head. "Used it all. I bought some more online. It doesn't help."

Of course it didn't. Ingredients to potions don't work nearly as well if a witch hasn't used her intention to make you well.

"Makes me wonder what else you put in there," Kate continued.

"Nothing. You never know what you're going to get if you order off the internet. My suppliers are either local people I trust, or people Trina trusted. I don't need to worry about the quality of anything I make."

She looked at me skeptically. "Other people do, though."

Palmer stood up, walked to Kate, and put a hand on her shoulder. "I think we've got everything we need here. Let's interview the landlord and the other tenants."

He turned back to me. "I'm posting an officer next door. Don't bother him, and don't get involved in the investigation. Let us do our job."

At the door, Kate turned to me. "And don't leave town for the next few days. We may have more questions for you."

Once they closed the apartment door, Jameson left my room and hissed.

Lisa Bouchard

"It's okay, they're just doing their job."

Chapter 6

I considered breakfast, but realized I couldn't eat. Poor Mrs. Thompson. She seemed so alive and vibrant just yesterday.

Mrs. Thompson would never get to go deal with the family problem she had. I guessed her family would have to work it out on their own. I wished she'd told me what the problem was—maybe I could have helped.

We'd never spend another night drinking tea and playing cribbage, either. I'd miss our time together. It's not often two women with over fifty years' age difference became friends, but we had. I had opened up to her, telling her how I saw my future, in a way I didn't want to tell my own mother or grandmother. Mrs. T. accepted whatever I had to say and didn't judge me.

Fat tears rolled down my cheeks. I reached for the box of tissues on the coffee table and Jameson jumped off my lap.

Why did another friend of mine have to die? It didn't seem fair. At least Mrs. T. went peacefully in her sleep. Grandma said these things come in threes, and I hoped she was wrong. I couldn't take another loss.

Jameson padded into the kitchen, stood by his bowl of water, and meowed.

I stood and joined him in the kitchen. "Do you need more water?" His bowl was not empty. "Maybe food?"

He'd need food and a litter box if I was going to leave him here for the day. "Hang on, I'll be right back."

I opened my apartment door and smiled at the officer in front of Mrs. Thompson's door. He was tall, and even younger than me, and looked like he ought to be in school, not guarding a potential crime scene. His uniform had the squeaky-new look Kate's had lost, and his rigid posture told me he took his responsibility to guard the door seriously.

"Hi. I'm Isabella."

His nametag read "Papatonis."

I held my hand out to him. "Nice to meet you, Officer Papatonis."

He nodded rather than shake my hand. "Ma'am. Is there a problem?"

Ma'am? There couldn't be more than three years' difference between the two of us. How dare he start off with ma'am? Then again, I hadn't seen myself in a mirror this morning, and I might look a little frightening—black hair pointing every which way. "Yes. I've got Mrs. Thompson's cat. She has me cat sit

40

when she leaves town, and so when I opened her door today, Jameson, the cat, ran to my door."

He looked confused. I'd take that over frightened.

"When I found Mrs. Thompson, I didn't even think to take anything for the cat. I've got to leave for work in a bit and don't want to leave him with no food or litter box."

He nodded. "I can see the problem."

"And I don't have time to run out and get supplies. Do you think I could go in and take a few cat things?"

He frowned. "I'm not allowed to let anyone in, except police."

I smiled what I hoped was my most disarming smile. "Oh, absolutely. I completely understand. It's just . . . the poor cat has lost his owner and now won't have food." I wrinkled my nose. "Or a litter box."

He shifted from foot to foot. "I sympathize, ma'am, really I do. I have a cat, too."

"Maybe you could get them for me?" I asked.

He looked happier about that idea.

"The food is in the cabinet under the sink, and the litter box and extra litter are in the bathroom. It would only take a minute, and I promise I won't let anyone in while you're inside."

Before he could reply, his phone rang. "Papatonis," he answered. After a moment, he said, "Yes, detective. Everything is fine here. There's a woman who wants to take cat supplies from the apartment. She lives next door. Should I let her in?"

After a moment, he handed his phone to me.

"Hello," I said.

"You have thirty seconds to go in, get what you need, and leave," Palmer said. "Papatonis will inspect everything you take out."

"Thank you. This is going to be much better for Jameson."

"And Ms. Proctor, don't snoop around." Ms.? What was it with guys today?

"I promise. Thank you."

I handed the phone to Papatonis, who listened to Palmer, then hung up. He unlocked the door for me. "Be quick."

He was trying to sound firm and authoritative, but it was hard to take him seriously when his voice almost cracked. I smiled and walked in. I made a beeline for the kitchen and grabbed Jameson's food and food bowl. I set them on the floor by the door and walked toward the bathroom. The door to Mrs. T.'s bedroom was closed. I looked at it and shivered. I glanced at Mrs. Thompson's desk, tempted to see what she had been writing the night before. I know I said I wouldn't snoop. Just taking a quick look wasn't snooping, was it?

The letter to Rosemarie was still on top of the papers. I took a quick picture of it and the addressed envelope next to it.

Papatonis opened the door a crack. "Do you need help?" he asked.

I scooted into the bathroom. "Yes, please. I won't be able to take everything in one trip by myself."

He opened the door the rest of the way. "What can I do?"

"If you take the food, I can manage the litter."

We brought the cat supplies out of the apartment. He stopped at my door. "I have to stay out here."

I set down the things I was carrying to take the food from him. "Thank you for your help."

I tried to close my door, but he said, "Wait."

I looked at him quizzically.

"I need to look through what you took." He peeked into the food bag and the litter container. "It's just a formality. I don't want to tell Detective Palmer I didn't follow orders."

"Of course. I understand. He's pretty intense sometimes."

We shared a smile before I brought Jameson's supplies into my apartment and closed the door. "Jameson, I've got food," I called out.

I scooped food into his bowl and put it in the kitchen, next to the water bowl. The litter box went next to the bathroom sink, just where it was in Mrs. T.'s apartment, so he would know where to find it. I looked at my watch. Eight thirty. I needed to get a move on.

Jameson ate, then found the sunny spot on the carpet in front of the living room window.

I grabbed my sandals, slipped my phone and keys into my pocket, and was surprised to see Jameson waiting for me at the apartment door.

"I can't let you go back home. The officer won't let you in. You're going to stay here today."

He didn't move.

"I've got to go. I need to open the shop."

Jameson tilted his head but didn't move.

I opened the door and tried to walk around him, but he walked out with me. I bent down to pick him up, but he scooted down the hallway.

"Problems with the cat?" Papatonis asked.

"It looks like he doesn't want to stay home alone."

"Poor little guy's had quite a shock. Maybe if I get around the other side of him, we can catch him."

I looked from Papatonis to Jameson. "No, I don't think that'll be necessary. You're right about him having a tough night. I'll bring him with me to work."

Jameson walked toward me.

"You going to carry him?" he asked.

I thought for a moment. As far as I knew, Jameson was an indoor cat, and I didn't want him to get lost, or worse, on the streets. He needed me to carry him.

"Just keep an eye on him while I go get a bag to carry him in."

I unlocked my door—honestly, with a policeman right next door and some heavy-duty wards, why did I bother—and got the pink-and-orange beach tote from my room.

Back out in the hall, Jameson was allowing Papatonis to pet him, but when he saw the bag, he hissed at me. Okay. Maybe we weren't going to use the bag. "No bag? How about a leash?" I asked Jameson.

It's not easy reading the expression on a cat's face, so I went back inside to get a length of ribbon. I had no idea if this would work as I hastily reviewed the knots I'd learned over a decade ago in scouts. I fashioned a quick harness around his chest and legs with the ribbon that I thought he couldn't escape from.

Jameson flopped over on the floor and lay still.

"Listen, if you want to come with me, it's either the bag or the leash. You pick."

He lifted his head off the floor and hissed at the bag. Apparently, he chose the leash, because he started walking to the stairs. "Okay then, leash it is," I said as I picked up the end and followed him down the stairs.

Once outside, Jameson paused and looked around, taking in the birds sitting on the telephone wire and the six dogs being walked by one woman. I was pretty sure the dogs weighed more than she did and was amazed she could keep them all behaving.

After the dogs walked by, Jameson started walking. He took the appropriate turns and led me to work. How had he known where to go? I was beginning to think he was no ordinary cat.

Chapter 7

I liked to get into work early enough to settle in before my first customers arrived. I had a routine to get ready for the day, and I hated it when I was rushed. I supposed, though, that the death of a friend and the sudden inheritance of a cat were good reasons to run late.

Jameson led me down the side of the building to the shared courtyard and back door of the apothecary. I checked the greenhouse door—still locked. Ordinarily I'd go in and water and take care of the plants. Starting my day with plants always made me happy. Today, I'd have to squeeze in greenhouse time when I could.

I picked up the packages stacked by my door. I hadn't finished replenishing the stock the shop lost, but I was getting close. A few more months, and I'd have everything I needed. With Jameson in front of me, I unlocked the door and walked in, balancing packages as I closed the door behind us. I stopped just inside and felt the familiar feeling of joy tinged with sadness. I loved owning the business and spending my days helping others, but the cost had been too high. I'd have given anything to go back to being Trina's apprentice.

I dropped the packages on a table in the prep room, hoping to have time to open them later on. I had to prepare for the day's customers.

"You'll be okay here," I told Jameson. "I've got a lot to do, but I'll be back once we open."

I moved the box of catnip to the top shelf, hoping he wouldn't be able to get to it. Jameson didn't look interested as he jumped onto Trina's work table, lay down, and began to lick his paws.

As always, the first thing I did was light the memorial candle that sat on the counter, next to a photo of Trina. "Good morning, Trina. I still miss you terribly." I knew if she were still here, together we could find something to help Agatha. I knew she couldn't hear me, but talking to her every day helped keep me focused. Dealing with customers who didn't like what you had to say was difficult, and I used Trina's lessons of kindness and compassion to steer me in the right direction.

I'd made a few changes to the apothecary over the past months. I now had a display of bagged teas in the front of the shop that were popular with tourists. My regular customers wanted loose leaf teas they could mix themselves, and tourists preferred prepackaged. I resupplied the tea table with mugs, sugar, and honey, then brewed some pomegranate oolong as the tea of the day. Trina loved all oolong teas, so it seemed a fitting remembrance to brew some each week in her memory.

Next, I unlocked the office and pulled the drawer to the cash register out of the newly installed safe. The wall safe was large enough to hold several potion books, the cash drawer, and a few expensive ingredients. After having dangerous potion recipes stolen, I vowed never to be put in that position again. Even without the additional potency a witch added to a potion, many of these could be quite harmful.

Out in the store, I put the cash drawer in the register and closed it.

I poured myself a mug of tea and walked through the store. I had tidied after I closed yesterday, but making sure everything was in its place was calming.

Once I made sure I hadn't missed anything last night, I went to the office and sat at the desk. I still hadn't finished choosing suppliers, but didn't have the mental strength to deal with so many choices yet. I pulled a piece of stationery from the desk drawer and thought for a moment. I wanted to write a short letter to Mrs. Thompson's son, letting him know how special she was to me and also that I had Jameson, if he wanted to claim him.

I bit my lip and started writing.

Dear Mr. Thompson,

I'm sorry we've never met. I was your mother's neighbor. I am very sorry for your loss. Your mother was a kind woman who helped my roommate and me out when we needed her.

Your mother has also been a friend to me, inviting me over for tea and cribbage, and I have watched Jameson for her when she was out of town. He is currently staying with me and if you'd like to pick him up, feel free to stop by.

I will miss your mother and her kindness terribly.

With deepest condolences,
Isabella Proctor

Short and simple. I hoped the letter would bring him some comfort. Mrs. T.'s passing reminded me that I shouldn't take Grandma for granted. I should make an effort to see her more, so I wouldn't regret missing time with her in the future.

I put the letter in the outgoing tray. I'd check with Palmer to make sure he'd been notified and ask for the address.

Thinking of envelopes and addresses reminded me of the photos I took of Mrs. Thompson's desk. I pulled out my phone and swiped to them.

The first photo was of the letter to Rosemarie. It wasn't finished, but it seemed she owed Mrs. Thompson five hundred dollars, and Mrs. T. needed to be repaid right away.

Five hundred dollars? Mrs. T. lived frugally, and I was surprised she had that kind of money to loan to a friend.

I swiped to the next picture: Rosemarie's name and address on an envelope. She lived on the other side of Portsmouth.

Lisa Bouchard

Was it possible Mrs. T. had been murdered for the money? I squeezed my eyes shut, then opened them.

There was nothing to say. Mrs. T. wasn't murdered, and I needed to slow my suspicious mind down.

The door chimes rang, and I left the office to greet my customer.

Mrs. Newcomb was looking at the display of scented candles I'd moved to the middle of the shop. I hadn't seen her for a week, and now I knew why. "Loving the new hair!"

She turned to me, and I realized her hair wasn't the only thing that had changed. "And look at you! You look great."

"Thanks, doll. I thought it was time, you know, to get back to looking nice. I spent yesterday at the spa—new haircut and color, a two-hour facial, and a massage that made me feel like I'd died and gone to heaven."

She'd had her long gray hair cut to shoulder length and colored a gorgeous shade of honey blonde. She'd abandoned the tight chignon she usually wore for loose waves. Her subtle makeup complemented the new hair nicely. "And what does Mr. Newcomb think?"

She laughed. "He's such a liar, he says I don't look a day over fifty."

I smiled. "He's not lying, you look fantastic."

"I don't know what's gotten into me, but I feel much better lately. I have so much more energy now that I'm not coughing and wheezing. I think it's your new tonic."

I'd never made Mrs. Newcomb's tonic before Trina passed, and I hadn't made any changes to Trina's recipe in the formulary. She wasn't the only customer to say they'd started to feel better now either.

"Enough about me, doll. How are you?"

"Not too bad." I didn't want to lie, but I didn't want to talk about Mrs. Thompson, either.

She gave me a skeptical look. "I'm shopping today, new clothes for the new me. I had to stop here first and show you how you've helped me. What's the tea for today?"

I pointed to the menu chalkboard on the wall that read "pomegranate oolong."

"Oh, I haven't tried that one yet." She cleared her throat but didn't cough. This was a definite change—usually, once she started, it took time for her to get a coughing fit under control.

I picked up a mug from the table. "Let me pour you some. With or without caffeine?"

"Definitely caffeinated. And with a touch of honey."

I made her tea and handed it to her. As I did, I used my intuition to see if there was anything I ought to offer her today. Her cough was doing much better, and she didn't need anything else.

"I know what you mean. I'm all caffeine until at least lunchtime, or I'll fall asleep by three."

She took a sip. "Delicious. Does it come in loose leaf or tea bags?"

"This is some of the tea bags. Can I get you some?"

She took another sip. "Absolutely."

I took a magenta tin off the shelf and handed it to her. "Are you looking for anything else in particular?"

"No, but we ought to talk, sweetie."

I'm not sure Mrs. Newcomb ever called people by their actual names. I liked her affectionate terms for me, even if I did think maybe she couldn't remember my name.

I raised an eyebrow. "About what?"

"Since you're not going to bring the topic up, I just heard your neighbor died in her sleep."

"Yes. Mrs. Thompson. She looked very peaceful when I found her."

"You saw her?"

"I did. Her cat was wailing, so I used my key to her apartment to see what was wrong."

"Oh, the poor dear. Where is the cat now? You didn't let the police take her to an animal shelter, did you?"

I smiled. "No. Jameson's a good cat, and I watched him whenever Mrs. T. went out of town. When I opened her door, he ran right to mine."

She nodded.

"Wait a minute, how did you hear about her?"

She took another sip of her tea. "Old lady gossip. Chloe Bickham saw the coroner parked at your building and watched for a little while. She figured out what apartment they were in and then started calling around with the news."

"I see. She ought to be part of the neighborhood watch."

"And now I find out you found her body. How terrible for you."

I looked down at my feet. I was sad at the loss of Mrs. T., but considering the relative peacefulness of her passing compared to Trina's, I wasn't quite so devastated.

"Well, it's never nice. At least she went in her sleep."

"Let me buy this tea and get out of your hair, doll. I've got a few calls to make. In her sleep, you say?"

I nodded. "I found her in bed, in her pajamas."

She paid for the tea and rushed out of the shop.

I made my way to the prep room to unbox the morning's deliveries of cinnamon bark, rose oil, and myrrh. "Adjusting to the life of shop cat?" I asked Jameson.

He hadn't moved since I left him, and he seemed to be fine.

I was daydreaming, thinking of other potions I could create, while I worked my way through making the week's orders. The door chimes rang, bringing me out of my reverie.

"Isabella?" Delia called.

I smiled and walked out of the prep room to see my cousins Delia and Thea carrying pizza and drinks.

We were cousins, and we looked like we were related, even though our styles were very different. Thea had a no-nonsense style, wore her long brown hair pulled back, and hardly ever wore makeup. Delia was the one who spent the most time on her looks—

blonde hair with red tips that matched her lipstick, perfect wings on her eyeliner, and clothes that were more stylish than Thea's jeans and T-shirts. I fit somewhere in the middle with nicer clothes, plain black hair, and rarely more makeup than a quick swipe of mascara and lip gloss.

I hadn't eaten anything today, and the smell of pizza made my stomach growl. "You read my mind. I'm starving."

They followed me into my office, where I cleared off the desk to make space for lunch. They'd brought my favorite pizza. I grabbed the first slice and took a large bite. The spicy sauce and crispy crust created the perfect foundation for the hot cheese, mushrooms, and onions. "Yum," I said once I swallowed. "You two are great."

Delia looked at me, brows furrowed. "Are you okay?"

I nodded. "I'm sad, but I'll be okay."

Thea handed me a bottle of iced tea.

"At least she went peacefully," Delia said.

"I suppose so. I wonder . . ."

"Oh no. Absolutely not. She died peacefully in her sleep, and that's all there is to it," Thea said.

I wasn't sure. "Would her apartment be guarded if she'd died in her sleep?"

"Guarded by who?" Delia asked.

"Palmer left an officer in front of the door. You don't do that unless you have suspicions and want to protect the crime scene."

Chapter 8

You saw Palmer today?" Delia asked.

I nodded.

"How'd that go?" Thea asked after she swallowed a bite of pizza.

"Is this the real reason you two came here? Looking for details of my nonexistent love life?" I didn't blame them; none of us had been particularly lucky in love.

"He was investigating a death, so there wasn't a lot of chitchat."

"Did he explain why he hadn't called you?" Delia asked.

"We didn't get into our personal lives. He asked about Mrs. Thompson, and I told him I had her cat," I said.

"You have Jameson? Lucky you!" Thea said.

We had wanted a pet when we were younger, but the aunts always said no. Not all witches have familiars. In fact, no one at Proctor House had one. The problem with having a pet was that a familiar wouldn't choose you if you had one.

"Do you think..." Thea said.

"I have no idea if Jameson was her familiar, and right now he's just a regular cat. He's in the prep room, napping."

"It could be..." Delia said.

"I don't even want to consider it right now," I said.

The other thing about having a familiar was it meant you were destined to be a powerful witch. I couldn't imagine being stronger than my aunts or grandmother, who didn't have familiars. I wasn't sure I was up for so much responsibility.

"Palmer didn't seem to mind that I took him, and I told him I'd check with her family to see if anyone else wanted him," I said.

I remembered something else he said too. "He also told me Kate hadn't forgiven me yet."

"Forgiven you for what?" Delia asked.

"Putting her to sleep," Thea said.

"Oh, right," Delia said. "Really? She's still upset?"

"Yeah. I'm not sure there's any more I can do."

I'd already apologized to her, but she wouldn't talk to me. And she wouldn't forgive me. I guess she didn't have to. I had the feeling that as long as she didn't forgive me, Palmer would be angry with me as well.

"Maybe now that you'll be seeing her more often, she'll see you as the good person you are, and she'll let it go," Thea suggested.

"I'm not sure I'll be seeing more of her, though. Palmer could pull the guard at any time. Besides, you didn't see how angry she looked when I offered her a cup of coffee this morning. She's going to take a while to forgive me."

My phone rang. I looked at the caller ID. "Speak of the devil," I said. "It's Palmer."

I answered the phone and walked out to the front window. "Hello, Detective."

"Good afternoon. I need to ask you a few more questions. Are you at work?"

"I am. I'll be here until six."

I hung up and filled my cousins in.

"We'll go so you can be alone with him," Thea smirked.

"That's not going to do me any good, you know," I said as they walked out of the office.

I heard the door chimes, and I assumed it was my cousins leaving, but I heard them say, "Hi, Aunt Michelle," and I knew I was doomed. My mother was here, and she only comes to my work when she's worried.

"I'm in the office," I called out to my mother.

She walked in and took a seat. My mother, at forty-nine, was stunning. Her black hair was starting to go gray in the front, framing her face with silver-white highlights.

"I just heard. I'm so sorry," she said.

I smiled. She was out of breath and must have rushed here to check on me. "Did you run?"

She shook her head. "No. I walked as fast as I could, though. Maybe I should take up jogging. I shouldn't be this out of shape. Anyway, how are you? Are you okay?"

Before I could answer, Jameson came in and jumped on the desk.

"You have a cat?" my mother asked.

"This is Jameson. He was Mrs. Thompson's, and when I found her, he came back with me to my apartment."

She held her hand out for him to sniff. My mother passed whatever cat test he had and was allowed to pet him.

"Is he yours now?" she asked.

It was beginning to look like it, but I didn't want to rush into anything. "I'm not sure. I've written to her son, and if he wants the cat, that will be the end of it."

Jameson hissed and jumped off the desk.

My mother sighed. "I don't know exactly how to ask this. Was her death a natural one?"

I leaned back in my chair and closed my eyes. "I don't know. It looked like she passed quietly in her sleep, but Palmer put a guard on her door."

"Detective Palmer is in charge of the case?"

I frowned. "And Kate's helping him. She's still mad at me."

"It may take her more time to come around. He's a good detective, and he'll figure out what happened."

And here it comes. Pleasantries out of the way, I prepared for the inevitable "you should move home" lecture.

"There's no reason for you to get involved. Just stay out of the investigation. Look at what happened to you and poor Abby last time. I don't think my nerves can take any more strain."

"You don't need to worry. I promise we'll be safe. In fact, I'm not sure we can be much safer than we are with an officer outside the next door over."

"Promise me. Don't stick your nose in where it doesn't belong."

"I promise, Mom."

What's that? Proctor witches didn't lie? Very true, but my mother had left me a huge loophole— who's to say where I, or my nose, truly belonged?

The door chimes rang again, and I stood up. "I'm sorry, I've got to get back to work."

My mother stood, too. "Of course. Come to dinner soon?"

She was now asking, instead of demanding, I come to dinner at Proctor House. That was a nice change she'd started after we caught Chuck.

"Soon. I promise." And this wasn't any kind of lie. It was much easier to say yes when she asked instead of ordered.

We walked onto the shop floor and saw Mrs. Newcomb. I waved to my mother as she left, and then turned to see how I could help my customer.

"Back so soon? What can I get you?" I asked her.

She smiled. "I'm still good, doll. But have I got some information for you. I thought you could pass it along to that handsome detective you ought to be dating by now."

I rolled my eyes. "We're not likely to be dating any time soon. He's a little upset with me because I've found another dead woman."

"Well, I'll tell you, it's a little concerning to me too. I worry someday it's going to be you that someone else finds."

I tried to smile reassuringly, but it was a thought in the back of my mind too. "You know us Proctor women, practically indestructible. So tell me, what's the scoop?"

She walked to the tea table and poured herself a mug of pomegranate oolong. "I don't know if it's true, but it's a doozy if it is."

I raised an eyebrow.

"I heard Beatrice had to leave the town she used to live in because the people there hated her, including her son. Not that I want to speak ill of the dead, but we have to consider there's more to her than the sweet old lady act she shows around town."

"Where did she come from?"

She took a sip of her tea. "Oh my, this is delicious. I'm glad I bought some earlier."

"Her town?"

"That's the funny thing. No one knows anything other than it's in the northern part of the state."

It had to be Sewall. The town was hidden from non-magic people, so it made sense no one could remember it.

"That's interesting, but I doubt there's much more we can find out, if we don't know the name of the town."

She finished her mug of tea and walked to the counter in the back of the shop. "I suppose not, but you have to agree, it does put her in a different light."

"It certainly does. Can I get you anything else this afternoon?"

"No, I don't think so. You are going to look into this, aren't you? You did such a bang-up job finding that despicable man who killed Trina. I'm sure you'll find this killer too."

I smiled. "I appreciate your confidence. Right now, we have no reason to believe anything bad happened to her. I hope to meet her son in the next few days, and I can at least ask him a question or two."

Chapter 9

Twenty minutes after Mrs. Newcomb left, Palmer walked through my door. I smiled at him, but he didn't smile back. Bats! Was he really this angry at me? I looked closer. He wasn't angry, he was worried. "Can I make you some tea?" I mentally smacked myself upside the head. "Maybe a bottle of water? Sealed and never been opened."

He picked up a quartz crystal from the gem table and rolled it in his palm. "No. I'm fine."

I put the feather duster I'd been using on the glass herb jars away behind the counter. "That's quartz. We use it in healing and it can help bring romance into your life."

He set the crystal down and furrowed his brow. "Do you believe in all that nonsense?"

Great. I guess I shouldn't have been surprised he would be so closed-minded. "I don't know. Tourists like buying crystals and some of them swear by their properties. I'm an herbalist, so I put my faith in the healing power of plants."

He looked along the herb wall, taking the time to read the label on each jar.

Jameson walked into the room, hissed at Palmer, and ran into my office.

"Are you looking for something in particular? If we don't have it, I can order anything you need."

"Do you carry aconite?"

I didn't recall ordering any aconite. Then again, I'd ordered a lot lately. "No, I don't think so. It's a flower, right?"

"Yes. Purple flowers."

"Have you notified Mrs. Thompson's next of kin?"

He turned to me. "Why?"

"I wrote him a short note, but didn't want to mail it until I was sure you'd talked to him first."

Palmer nodded. "How well do you know him?"

"I've never met him. Writing a note is just the kind of thing you do, if you don't know someone well enough to visit."

I scanned the herbs: agrimony, alder buckthorn, angelica. Aconite would have been first on the shelf, but I had none. "What do you need it for?" I asked.

"Maybe you have some out back?"

I shook my head. "Anything in the prep room has a corresponding jar out front."

"How about the greenhouse?"

I pursed my lips. "Definitely not. I just finished buying the plants to replace the dead ones and I didn't buy aconite."

"Mind if I take a look?" he asked.

I didn't mind, but I wanted to know what was going on. "Does this have to do with Mrs. Thompson?"

"I can't talk about an ongoing investigation. Can I go out to the greenhouse, or do you want me to come back with a warrant?"

That sounded like a detective's way of saying yes without actually saying yes. I stared into his eyes, trying to determine whether I needed to call a lawyer. I thought Palmer was an honest guy, but if he was holding a grudge on Kate's behalf, I worried. "Am I in some kind of trouble?"

"Not if you don't carry aconite," he said.

I pulled my phone out of my pocket and did a quick google search. I felt the blood drain from my face as I read the poisonous effects the plant had. "I need to sit down."

He followed me to my office and perched on the arm of one of the visitor's chairs.

I took a few deep breaths. "You can't possibly believe I'd hurt Mrs. Thompson."

"I don't want to. Believe me. I think you're a fundamentally good person. You've got history, though, and I'm not about to trust your word."

That stung. His words hurt more because I'd earned them. Even though there was a big difference between a tea that helped you sleep and a deadly poison, I could see from the set of his jaw that he thought if I'd do one, I'd do the other.

"Go ahead. I've got nothing to hide."

He pulled out his phone and said, "You got that?"

The door to the apothecary opened and I stood.

"That's my team. We'll stay in here, out of their way."

My stomach sank. He had a team—he had been prepared. At least part of him thought I'd killed Mrs. Thompson.

There was a single knock at the office door. "The greenhouse is locked," Papatonis said.

Palmer held his hand out. "I'll take the key to the greenhouse."

I handed him the spare key I kept in my desk, and he handed it to Papatonis.

"I'll search in here, if you don't mind."

"Okay," I said in a small voice.

He pulled on gloves and moved through the room, quickly and professionally searching every inch. I stood in the corner while he went through the desk.

"Do you have the combination?" he asked, looking at the safe.

I opened the safe for him. "There are expensive ingredients in here, so please be careful."

He took the few small jars out of the safe and placed them on the desk. Then he took my copy of *Drostov's Book of Potions and the Healing Arts* and flipped through it. "Potions?" he asked.

"Potions is an old word for tincture or herbal cure. Half the teas we drink now were once considered potions."

"And the love spells are missing?"

65

"Torn out when Trina died. They're in a folder at the bottom of the safe."

There was a knock at the door. The officer who arrived first when I found Trina looked in at us. "Hey, boss. I think I've found something."

"Come with me," Palmer commanded.

We walked into the prep room, where a bag of dried echinacea flowers had been emptied onto the table. I had to give the police credit, everything else had been returned to the shelves—in the wrong places—but put back neatly nonetheless.

"That's echinacea," I said.

The officer, whose name was O'Neill, looked at the label of the bag they'd come from. "That's what the label says, but you said any purple flower."

Palmer held his hand out, and O'Neill handed him the bag. He looked at me. "What's this for?"

"Echinacea and goldenseal boost the immune system. Most people drink echinacea and goldenseal tea when they feel a cold coming on."

Palmer pulled up a picture of echinacea on his phone and compared it to the dried flowers.

"This isn't what we're looking for. Pack this up. Did you find anything else in here?"

"No," O'Neill said.

Palmer walked out to the sales floor and I followed him. "Nothing here, boss," Kate said.

Her expression hardened when I stepped out from behind him to look at my shop. As in the prep room, things had been put back on a shelf, though not the correct one. I knew what I'd be doing for the rest of the afternoon.

Palmer turned to me. "Let's talk in your office."

He followed me in and closed the door. He sat and said nothing, looking at me.

Out the window, I saw officers in the greenhouse. They were unlikely to do any damage there, because it seemed like Palmer had told them to be careful. I didn't feel I owed him an explanation for things I hadn't done and resolved to wait him out.

Finally, he said, "You're a bright woman. You've put together that Mrs. Thompson has been poisoned. The ME almost missed it, except for the irritation at the back of her mouth."

Bats! Thea was not going to be happy about this. "Who would have wanted to kill her? She didn't have much to steal, and I can't imagine she'd made anyone that mad at her."

"We don't know." His phone rang. "Yes. Right, okay," was all he said. "That was the other search team. Abby let them into your apartment, and they didn't find anything there, either."

Anger flashed through me. "Of course they didn't. I'm not a murderer, and you know that. The chief knows it, too."

"I want to believe you, but . . ." he drifted off.

"For crying out loud! It was a tea that let Kate fall asleep a little easier. Maybe if she wasn't spending all her free time doing extra work for you, she wouldn't have fallen asleep. Did you ever consider that?"

His eyes narrowed. I'd hit a nerve. Good.

"Regardless, you gave her something and didn't tell her."

"Don't be ridiculous. She knew she was drinking tea."

"It's a matter of trust, Ms. Proctor. Once lost, trust is very difficult to regain."

I took a deep breath and steeled myself for his answer to my question. "Is there anything I can do to regain your trust?"

He frowned. "I don't know. It's going to take a long time, and I can't guarantee anything."

"Fine. Let's move on. Other than me, do you have any suspects?"

He snorted. "I don't discuss ongoing investigations with members of the public. You can read about it in the paper like everyone else."

He was so infuriating! "Alright then. If you don't mind, I've got a shop to put back in order. I'm sure you can see yourself out."

He looked perplexed. "I told them to be careful and not make a mess."

I sighed. "I appreciate that, I really do. While everything is back on shelves and neat, nothing is in the right place."

He stood. "I'll let you get to it, then. But first, how many other herbalists are there in the Portsmouth area?"

"I'm the only one."

How about the rest of your family?"

"My grandmother and the aunts know enough to get by, but if you think they'd poison anyone, you're wrong."

Chapter 10

I closed the shop early, something I never do, and practically ran home, with Jameson keeping up with me.

Officer Papatonis was still stationed outside Mrs. Thompson's door. "Busy day?" I asked him.

"Not for me. I just stood here."

I tried to reach my senses into Mrs. Thompson's apartment, searching for hints of magical malfeasance, but I felt nothing. Not even the residual magic you'd feel in any witch's home. Something was masking the magic in her apartment. Papatonis looked at me. "Are you okay?"

"Yeah, I was thinking. She didn't deserve to be poisoned by someone so close to her."

I waited to see if he would say anything useful. He responded with, "I wouldn't know anything about that, ma'am."

Oy! Again with the ma'am.

Lisa Bouchard

As soon as I unlocked the door, Abby started apologizing. "I'm sorry, Isabella. I didn't know what to do, and I was sure you didn't keep anything bad here, so I said yes. Are you in any trouble?"

Abby was a ball of nervous energy. Her hair was coming out of its braid, a sure sign she'd been tugging at it while the apartment was being searched.

I kicked off my sandals and said, "Hey, don't worry. I'm here and everything is okay. First, did they take anything?"

She shook her head. "No."

We sat at the dining table. "Did they tell you Mrs. Thompson was poisoned?" I asked.

"They didn't tell me anything."

"She was poisoned with a plant I never work with, precisely because it's poisonous."

Her brow creased. "I don't like this. Another murder, and this time even closer to home."

I squeezed her hand. "Hey, don't worry. This has nothing to do with us. We're just unlucky enough to live next door. And right now we've got the safest apartment in town, with the officer standing guard."

"All the same, I think we should get the alarm system you wanted."

I squeezed her hand again. "Tell Mr. Subramanian, and he'll have it installed." I didn't actually care about the alarm system, because the wards I'd put on the apartment would keep anyone from hurting either of us, as long as they were activated. Now that Abby had agreed to the alarm system, though, she'd keep the door shut, and the wards would remain activated.

"I'm going to go talk to the officer outside for a minute."

I went out to the hallway. "I have a huge favor to ask you."

Papatonis frowned.

"I didn't take any of the cat's toys or his scratching post. He's already started going after my couch, and if I could get inside for one quick minute . . ."

"Absolutely not."

"Please? We can do it like before. You can check anything I take out."

"Miss Proctor, please. I can't. An hour ago you were a suspect in a murder investigation. You might still be a suspect for all I know. I can't let you into the crime scene."

I frowned. "Of course. I wasn't thinking."

As if on cue, Jameson howled inside my apartment. *Good boy!*

Papatonis frowned. "You stay here. I'll see if I can find you something. But nothing from the bedroom."

I grinned. "Absolutely. You're the best."

He unlocked the door and peered into the apartment.

"The scratching post is right by the window, in the office," I said.

As soon as he opened the door, I opened my senses wide and felt a wallop of dark magic. I hadn't felt this the other two times I was in the apartment. I tried to tease apart the different magic that had been used in the apartment lately, and I could feel the remnants of a blocking spell. I couldn't see who had poisoned Mrs. Thompson, but I could feel the persuasion spell they had used and feel the murky magic in the potion they'd put in her dinner.

I shut my senses down as Papatonis walked through the door.

"You okay?"

"Yes. I guess knowing someone wanted to hurt her has upset me more than I realized." I took the scratching post. "Thank you, you've really helped me out."

He nodded. "Maybe we don't have to tell Detective Palmer about this."

I put my fingers to my lips as though I were zipping them shut. "The secret is safe with me."

I set the post down in the living room. Jameson was far too well-mannered to scratch at my couch, but Papatonis didn't need to know that.

Abby was in the kitchen, flipping a grilled cheese sandwich over in the frying pan. "Hungry?" she asked.

It smelled delicious. Unfortunately, the residual evil magic next door had turned my stomach. "No. I had pizza with Thea and Delia earlier."

I walked into my bedroom and closed the door. Abby would worry when she heard me talking to my cousins about investigating Mrs. Thompson's murder.

Jameson had followed me in and he jumped up on my bed. I sat next to him and stroked his back.

I heard my name faintly. I stood up and opened my door. "Abby, did you call me?" I asked.

"No. I'm still throwing some dinner together. Are you sure you don't want any?"

"Oh, thanks. But no. I'm going out with Thea and Delia." Maybe I'd eat later on.

I went back to my bed, closed my eyes and listened, but heard nothing.

I called Delia, because I knew she'd help talk Thea into helping me find Mrs. T.'s killer.

"Are you ready to admit we need to investigate yet?" she asked.

I had to smile. "Yes. You should feel the evil magic left in the apartment. It's only there if you search for it when the door is open. Something horrible happened in there, and I'm worried Palmer and Kate can't handle it on their own."

"Okay, what's the plan?"

"First, we need to get Thea on board."

I heard the floorboards creak as Delia walked down the hallway to Thea's room. "You're on speaker with both of us now."

"Don't say no right away," I started.

Thea had never been one to do as I told her. "No. Absolutely not. We are not getting into another murder investigation."

"They aren't ready for this kind of magic. Some magical thug could roll right over them, killing as many people as they wanted."

I waited for a moment and then continued. "And I don't want that on my conscience. Do you?"

"I don't," Delia chimed in.

"I've got one clue. A woman owed Mrs. T. money, and I've got her address."

"Pretty weak, if you ask me," Thea said.

"Fine. Delia and I will go without you."

Thea sighed theatrically, and I knew I'd won. "We'll all go, and I'll drive."

"We'll talk to this one person. Anything that comes up has to go straight to Palmer," Thea demanded.

I raised an eyebrow. "Since when do you tell me what to do?" I asked.

"Since we have to hide what we're doing from the aunts. It's not easy, you know. They can sniff out a lie from a mile away, and they don't play fair. They gang up on us."

I laughed. "You'll be fine. Don't worry."

Chapter 11

I was up and ready to meet Thea and Delia outside the next morning. They had recently bought themselves a red Kia Sorento and would take any excuse to drive it. The car was big enough to hold our entire family, and I didn't think it would be long before they suggested we all go on vacation together so they could drive more. I slid into the middle seat and said, "527 Marsh Pond Lane."

Delia pulled out her phone and typed the address into a navigation app.

I sat back so she wouldn't see me roll my eyes. We were only going across town; they didn't need directions.

Thea pulled out of the parking lot. "What happened with Palmer?"

I took a breath and wondered how a used car could still have that new car smell. "He searched my apartment and the apothecary for poison," I said.

Thea looked at me in the rearview mirror.

"What?" Delia exclaimed.

"Mrs. Thompson was poisoned with a plant, and I was his first suspect."

"No way!" Thea said, her eyes back on the road.

"Yeah. I may never live down the sleepy tea incident. Can you believe he said he can't trust me?"

"There's a huge difference between tea and poison," Delia said.

"I know, right? Not in his mind. I yelled at him after he couldn't find anything, trying to explain the difference between allowing someone to relax a little bit and poisoning them."

"Good," Thea said. "He should know better than to accuse you."

I thought so, too. But as angry as I was with him, deep down I knew he had a point, and that I wouldn't feel right until I'd somehow regained his and Kate's trust.

Rosemarie's house wasn't far. I hadn't called first, and I hoped she would be home. We pulled into the driveway of the mid-century three-story colonial, and Delia whistled. "Nice house."

It certainly looked like the people who lived there could afford to repay Mrs. Thompson. We got out of the car and walked to the front door. I looked at the doorbell camera and said, "Hello?"

"Who is it?" an older woman's voice responded.

"Good afternoon, Mrs. Flagg. I'm a friend of Beatrice Thompson, and I was wondering if I could have a word with you," I said.

"One moment," she said.

She opened the door, but did not ask us to come in. "You're friends of Beatrice?" she asked skeptically.

"Yes, I'm her next-door neighbor. I wonder if you heard the news," I said.

"News?"

"Yes. Sadly, she passed recently."

Rosemarie looked genuinely surprised. "Well, then. I guess you should come in." She opened the door for us, and we followed her in.

The entry had marble floors and a stunning chandelier. The round table under the chandelier had a three-foot-tall arrangement of roses, delphinium, orchids, and greens. Beside the arrangement was a fact sheet about the house and several real estate business cards. The living and dining rooms looked as though they had been professionally decorated.

"Do you like the flowers?" she asked. "I'd be happy to make you up an arrangement for a small fee."

"They are lovely," I said. I leaned in to smell the roses and was disappointed to find they were not real.

She led us to a small study. "Please, have a seat."

We sat in the comfortable leather chairs.

"You say she's gone?" Mrs. Flagg asked.

I nodded. "Yes. In fact, I found her. And while I was in her apartment, I saw a letter she had started writing to you." I pulled out my phone and showed it to her.

Her eyes went wide. "I see. Well, this is embarrassing."

"Where were you two nights ago?" I asked.

"I beg your pardon?" she exclaimed.

"You owed her money, and I thought perhaps you couldn't pay her back."

She looked confused for a moment. "Oh, yes, I guess I do owe her a little bit of money."

"Could you tell us why you didn't repay her?" Thea asked.

"Honestly, I forgot. We'd gone out shopping. She didn't have a car, so I asked her to come with me to the outlets. Silly me, I forgot my wallet at home, and she offered to loan me money so it wasn't a wasted trip."

I nodded, not sure if I believed her, because the smile on her lips hadn't reached her eyes.

"I bet she suddenly needed that money because her landlord raised her rent again."

"Mr. Subramanian?" I asked.

"Yes. The last time we had brunch, she complained that he kept raising her rent."

"Is that legal?" Delia asked.

"I don't know. He hasn't said anything about raising my rent," I said.

"Beatrice talked him into renting to her at a low rate without any lease, so he's been incrementally raising the rent every month. She's paying almost two thousand a month now."

We weren't paying much less than that, but Abby and I each had a job. "Did she say why he kept raising the rent?"

She shook her head. "She never told me."

"Your house is lovely. I bet your backyard is wonderful. Do you mind if we look outside?" Delia asked.

I was confused at her non sequitur, but decided to go with it.

"I would love to show you the yard. My late husband was quite the gardener. I hate to give up all his hard work."

She brought us outside, and we were amazed at the riot of color in her husband's garden.

"Oh! How beautiful. Our grandfather would have loved this garden," I said.

"Thank you. Jeremiah spent a lot of time out here, making everything perfect."

I walked to a rosebush pruned to look like a tree. "Did he do the topiary work as well?" I asked.

Rosemarie nodded.

I brought my nose closer to the red roses and inhaled deeply.

"Would you mind if I took a few photos? For ideas for our family garden," Thea asked.

"Of course not," she said. "It's nice to have other people enjoying the garden again."

Thea pulled her phone out of her pocket, walked along the stone path that divided the garden in two, and began snapping photos. Out of the corner of my eye, I saw she was photographing every type of plant individually. Delia walked around the edge of the garden, looking down at the dirt.

Thea and Delia rejoined us. "Thank you for making the time to speak with us. We're sorry for your loss," I said.

"If you see Beatrice's son, please give him my condolences," she said.

"Did you find any clues?" I asked the two of them, once we were in the car.

"I found footprints in the dirt that I pointed out to Thea," Delia said.

Thea started the car and pulled out of the driveway. "The footprints are near some purple flowers, and I've got photos of the prints and the flowers."

I held my hand out. "Let's see."

Delia handed Thea's phone to me, and I looked at the picture. "Looks a lot like what Palmer was looking for," I said.

"Flip to the next picture," Thea said.

The next picture showed several of the aconite stems stripped of their flowers. "Oh, broomsticks! Do you think we found Mrs. T.'s killer?" I asked.

"A lot of flowers were cut, so it may mean nothing," Thea said.

"Good thing she didn't offer us anything to drink," Delia said.

"Did you see her face when we told her the news? She looked genuinely surprised. I don't know if she did it," I said.

Thea smiled. "Good. That's that, then. You can call Palmer and tell him what we found, and you can leave the rest of the investigation to him."

"We can't give up now," I said. "We at least need to look into my landlord."

"Absolutely not. I said one person. We're done," Thea said as she stopped at a stop sign.

I looked to Delia.

"No, don't put me in the middle of this. I can never choose between the two of you," she said.

"Fine. I'll talk to him on my own after work. Can you drop me at the apothecary?"

Thea looked back at me, exasperated.

"Just because he has a key to her apartment and had a reason to be angry with her doesn't mean he'd do anything to me," I said.

"I'm not leaving Isabella to investigate alone," Delia said.

Thea capitulated. "Fine. But this is it."

Chapter 12

I had too much to think about to go directly home after work. I wasn't ready to confront my landlord about being a possible murder suspect, because if I didn't handle it well, he might ask me to move. I walked the few blocks to Prescott Park instead. The park was between the Piscataqua River and Strawbery Banke, and usually had a cool breeze. It's always been the place I've gone to think. Walking among the plants, some of which were as old as the town, always relaxed me and allowed me to put my problems in focus. As I walked through the park, enjoying the flowers, I thought about everything that was bothering me. How had my life gotten that complicated? One year ago I was living at home, apprenticing at the apothecary, with what now seemed like the minor problem of an overprotective family.

Suddenly, I owned the apothecary, which was a struggle to run properly because there was so much I didn't know. I'd just found my second murdered friend and I managed to annoy my contacts in the police department badly enough that I couldn't get any information from them. Oh, and my family was so overprotective, I felt like I shouldn't tell them what was going on, to keep their blood pressures down.

The rhododendrons were in full bloom, and I bent down to inhale their sweet fragrance. The ones I had in my greenhouse had bloomed a month ago, along with the peonies, and it was nice to smell this one on its own.

I straightened up, turned around, and ran smack into Palmer. Great. He was the last person I wanted to see. I was out there to calm my mind, not get into an argument about investigating Mrs. Thompson's death.

"Oh, excuse me. I didn't see you," I said.

Palmer put his hand on my elbow to steady me. "Not a problem."

I think this was the first time I'd seen him in such casual clothing. He was wearing worn jeans, a T-shirt, and sneakers. Generally, I thought a man looked good in a suit, but he looked just as good today. This was about to get awkward with me gawking at him. Best to press on with some small talk. "I didn't take you for a person who would enjoy the park."

He arched an eyebrow. "Really? I find it relaxes me and helps me clear my mind. I usually come here when I'm stuck on a case. By the time I leave, I've usually got at least one new avenue to investigate."

Good to know he was as stuck as I was. I gestured to the path and started walking, happy he joined me. "And what are you stuck on tonight?"

"I don't discuss ongoing investigations," he said.

I grinned. By this point in the previous case, he had me in an interrogation room, accusing me of murder. This seemed like a step up. I worried for him, though. This murder involved magic, and he wasn't equipped to deal with that. "I get the feeling this case is more complex, and possibly more dangerous, than Trina's murder."

He nodded. "I agree. It takes a coldness to . . ."

I looked over at him. "Yes?"

"Not sharing information with members of the public," he reminded me.

"Of course not," I agreed.

"Since we're here, I wanted to ask you about how you found Abby in Chuck's trunk. Off the record."

I wondered if he was going to ask about what happened the night we found Trina's killer. We were all as vague as possible when he took our statements. The story couldn't have made much sense to him—four women out walking happened to run across him. "It's hard to explain," I began. At least it was hard to explain without telling the entire truth. Palmer was far from having my trust with my family secrets. "It was mostly Mrs. Thompson, honestly. She thought we should try to follow where someone might have gone without being caught by the officer you had stationed out front, so we went out the basement door, through the backyard and the trees, and came out on the street behind the building. At that point, she picked a direction and started walking. Honestly, it was pure luck that we noticed Chuck's car pulling into the 7-Eleven."

"How did you know he was the killer?"

"We didn't. He stopped in for beer, saw us walking toward him and panicked. A guy doesn't panic when buying beer unless there's something wrong."

I almost stumbled. Palmer was testing me. I told him all this when he took my statement. Thea and Delia had repeated a similar story to him that day as well. I understood why he didn't trust me about Kate's tea, but it was upsetting that he thought I was keeping something from him about Abby's kidnapping.

Then again, I *was* keeping something from him. Were his instincts so good that he could tell? Was I going to have to ask the chief to get him to back down?

Palmer nodded. "He gave himself away?"

"He did. Once we had him, he started talking and wouldn't stop. He confessed to killing Trina, and we found Abby in his trunk."

"I've been meaning to ask you about that, too. He swore he saw Trina's ghost, and he said he only confessed because she was threatening him. Do you know anything about that?"

I frowned. "Are you seriously asking me if I know anything about ghosts?"

Palmer laughed. "I guess not. But he was genuinely afraid."

"It sounds like a guilty conscience. Unless you believe in ghosts and spooky things that go bump in the night?"

"Not likely. I see enough bad in life without having to borrow trouble from the imaginary supernatural world."

"I agree."

He stopped at an Italian ice stand. "I find the lemon-lime is particularly good for thinking. Can I get you one?"

I smiled. This was nice, and I could get used to it. "Watermelon, please."

He ordered and paid, then we started walking again.

"Mrs. Thompson was your friend, and I know how much you want to get involved, but"—he stopped walking—"don't."

I stopped and looked at him. Had he already talked to Rosemarie, and had she told him we'd beaten him there? "Why would you—"

"Because I saw your face when you caught Chuck. Because I'm a good judge of character, and I know you want to do the right thing, and help, and keep people safe." He sighed. "You're a protector. But you're not trained, and you could get hurt."

"You could get hurt, too."

"The difference is, I'm trained for the job and you're not. I don't want to see you hurt, or worse. Let me do my job. I'm paid for the danger."

Interesting. He sounded more concerned than angry. "I didn't realize you cared so much. Does this mean you've forgiven me for giving Kate sleepy tea?"

"Absolutely not. And that's just what I mean. You were reckless—Kate could've helped you if you ran into trouble. No, wait. Kate could have called me, and I would have gone out instead."

I laughed. "If Chuck had driven right past you, you wouldn't have given him a thought. You said yourself he wasn't even on your radar. There's no way you were going to find him in time to save Abby."

"We would've found him, eventually. And it didn't look like he was going to kill her."

I scowled at him. "You know better than that. The minute she started complaining about being held prisoner, he would have slipped right into 'If I can't have her, no one can,' and then it's a quick hop to a murder-suicide."

"Stop!" he commanded. "You can't Monday-morning quarterback your way through an investigation to show how you were right. The bottom line is that civilians cannot get involved in police work, not unless they have specific skills we need. If I needed to put someone to sleep, you'd be the first person I called, but until I do, you need to step away and let me do my job."

"What makes you think I'm doing anything?"

"Because you haven't denied it. If you weren't investigating, you'd have said so when I first told you to stop. You didn't."

Busted. Probably best to keep not saying anything, because I didn't want to lie to him.

"Just as I suspected. And as for forgiving you, I can't. Not until Kate does."

I sighed. "It doesn't look like that's going to happen. I've called, I've tried talking to her in person, and she's so angry that I can't get through to her."

"Of course she's angry. Her job is to protect others and catch bad guys. You didn't let her protect you, and then you went out and caught a murderer. You took away everything she does."

Oh, broomsticks! I'd never considered that. "Now I feel really horrible. I hadn't looked at it from that perspective."

"Yeah. You've got a lot to make up for."

We walked for a few minutes in silence, eating our Italian ice.

"There is one way to solve all your police-related problems, you know."

"There is?"

"Yes. Join the force. The chief wants you to, and you'd be able to hunt down murderers to your heart's content."

"I doubt I'd get the chance. I'd be like poor Papatonis, standing in front of an empty apartment all day, keeping people like me out."

Palmer laughed. "At least for a while, yes, but eventually…"

Eventually could mean almost anything. "I'll stick with the apothecary."

"Then make sure I don't see you at any more crime scenes."

We were at the end of the park, and I saw his car.

"Can I give you a ride home?" he asked.

"No, thanks. It's a nice night, and now I've got more to consider than when I got here."

He climbed into his car and rolled his window down. "I meant what I said. I'm sure you can at least get Kate to not hate you, eventually."

He drove off, and I wasn't so sure he was right. I also knew there was no way I could abandon my investigation—he wasn't prepared for magic, and for as much as he thought he was protecting me, I knew I needed to protect him.

Chapter 13

When I got back to the apartment, a different officer stood guard at Mrs. Thompson's door. I'd never met her, so I just nodded and said hi before I unlocked my door and read the note Mr. Subramanian left in his distinctive handwriting.

Your new alarm system has been installed. Please change the code once you get home.

That was fast. I walked in and heard beeping to the right of the door. I looked at the alarm, panicked because I didn't know the combination. Mr. S. had left a sticky note with the numbers 0 1 2 3 printed on it.

I typed in the code, and the beeping stopped.

"Abby, you home?" I called out.

The only answer was Jameson poking his head out of my room and meowing. I smiled as I picked him up and nuzzled his neck. "Who's a good cat?" I asked.

Apparently not him, because he jumped out of my arms and made a beeline for the bathroom.

I pulled out my phone and texted Abby, asking what she wanted for dinner. She responded, saying she was at her parents' and would be back later tonight.

That was probably not good. Her parents would have heard about Mrs. Thompson's passing, and their worry for Abby, which had just started to subside after the kidnapping, would be ramped up again.

I opened the fridge and pulled out two slices of pizza left over from lunch yesterday. Jameson padded into the kitchen and meowed. I put more food in his bowl before I went to the couch and watched Rogue One, waiting for Abby to get home.

Partway through Episode IV, Abby finally came home. She heard the beeping and looked confused.

"We've got a new alarm system. The code is right there."

She punched in the code, and the beeping stopped again. "Kind of easy to guess," she said.

"We can change the code to whatever we want. You pick the code and tell me what it is."

She typed in a new code. "0904," she said.

I smiled. That was the day we met, way back on the first day of kindergarten. "Easy to remember, but I doubt anyone else knows how important it is for us."

She flopped down next to me on the couch and looked at the frozen tv image of two suns setting on Tatooine. "Four?" she asked.

I nodded. As much as she claimed she didn't like science fiction, she could correctly name any Star Wars movie from just about any scene. Maybe that was my fault—or should I let myself off the hook and say influence instead?

"You're out late tonight. Are your parents okay?" I asked.

"I've got tomorrow off. My parents are the same as always. Worried, thinking you're a bad influence, trying to bribe me to come home."

"Anything good?"

"A car."

My eyes widened. They weren't fooling around anymore. They wanted her home. "Did you take them up on it?" I asked.

She shook her head. "Nah. I don't need a car. Besides, we have an alarm system and an officer next door, we're safe here."

She watched the rest of the movie with me and then we went to bed.

I closed my eyes and willed my body to relax. I'd been holding a lot of tension and wouldn't fall asleep until I let it all go. Jameson jumped up on my bed and settled beside me, his paw gently resting on my cheek. My eyes grew heavy and I drifted off to sleep.

It seemed like only moments later that I awoke with a start. I heard breaking glass and looked to my window. The moon wasn't out, and I couldn't see anything. I reached behind me to turn on my lamp. Light flooded the room, and I saw a person on the porch roof, breaking the glass in my window. He cleared all the glass from the pane below the window latch.

I was frozen with fear. Who was this, and what did they want?

I watched as they tried to put their hand through the frame, but they couldn't.

"What?" a man's raspy voice said.

He tried again, but could not penetrate the ward on the window. "What's going on here?"

I was safe! My ward was holding. "Who are you?" I said, more shakily than I wanted to. He had a black balaclava on, and I couldn't make out any of his features.

"Let me in," he said with a snarl.

I threw my blanket off me, stood up and walked closer to the window. I didn't get too close, because I didn't want to cut my feet on the glass. "What do you want?"

Magic tingled across my skin, but if he couldn't get in, I didn't want to use it on him.

With one last surge of effort, he tried to push his hand through the hole he made in my window, and failed. Jameson hissed at him from the bed as the would-be intruder jumped off the roof.

There was a knock at my bedroom door. "Isabella, are you okay?" Abby asked.

How was I going to explain this to her? "Uh, yeah. I'm fine."

"What was that noise?"

I didn't mind not telling the whole truth, but I wasn't going to lie to her. "It's no big deal. You can go back to sleep."

"I'm opening the door," she said as she turned my door handle.

"What happened?"

"Be careful, there's broken glass on the floor."

She looked to the window, then to me. "Call Palmer."

Right. Call the police. That's what people did when their homes were broken into. I sat back on my bed and picked up my phone. Most people probably didn't have a police detective in their favorites, but I did.

"Palmer," his groggy voice answered.

"Hi, ah . . ." I trailed off.

"What's wrong? Are you okay?" His voice snapped to wakefulness.

"Someone tried to break into my apartment. I think they're gone now."

"I'll be right there."

Eight minutes later I saw flashing blue lights, and it took another thirty seconds for Palmer to pound on my door. I let him in, saying, "Shhh. Don't wake the neighbors."

He scowled. "Show me where he broke in."

I brought him to my room, and he looked out the window. "Be careful," he warned, "I don't want you to cut your feet. Nobody out there right now. Kate's doing a sweep of the neighborhood."

Great. Kate was here. "I don't have anything to fix the window with," I said.

"Your landlord should take care of the damage. Did you call him?"

I shook my head. "Not yet."

"Why would someone want to break in here?" Palmer asked me.

My heart hadn't stopped racing yet. "I don't know. I don't keep anything valuable here—I mean, look around. It doesn't even look like stealing my wallet would be worth the time." Maybe I was doing my bedroom a disservice, but honestly, I had nothing expensive here. I lived within my means, and while I was fairly good at saving money, the occasional emergency kept my savings account below four figures.

Palmer appraised my bedroom. "I see what you mean."

Ooof. That was rough. It's one thing to say you don't have much, but entirely another when a guy looks around and is unimpressed.

I reached for my phone. "I'll call the landlord."

Mr. Subramanian was in my apartment in under two minutes. "Are you girls alright?"

"Yes. I woke up before he could get in, and I guess that scared him off." There was no need to tell him the real reason the intruder couldn't make it in — my wards. I wondered if the broken window would weaken them. I wasn't sure, but there would be no harm in reworking them after everyone left.

"Where's Abby?" Mr. Subramanian asked.

"She's in her room." She was probably terrified. I wasn't sure she was completely over her kidnapping, and this attempted break-in certainly wouldn't help.

I knocked on her door. "Abby? Are you awake?"

She let me into her room. It was as tidy as ever, with the exception of a half-packed overnight bag on her bed. "We're going to be okay," I reassured.

She bit her lip. "I don't believe you. I don't feel safe here, and I want to go home."

I pulled her into a hug. "I know. The police are here, and I'm sure Palmer will post someone in the parking lot for the rest of the night. There's an officer in the hall already. Tonight, this might be the safest place in town."

"You say that like we haven't had two different break-ins in just three months."

"I know, I know."

"Is it too much to ask to feel safe in my own apartment?" she asked.

"Of course not. And I think we'll all feel much better once the sun comes up. A few more hours of sleep, and we can figure out what to do next."

She looked at me skeptically. "It would take a minor miracle for me to get back to sleep."

"I've got tea," I said.

"No bergamot?"

I smiled. "Never for you. Come with me to the kitchen, and I'll make some."

In the kitchen, I could hear Palmer and Mr. Subramanian talking in my room. "The city has to do better at protecting these girls. They can't keep having people break into their apartment. I've done my part and installed an alarm system."

"I've got officers searching for the intruder, and I'll have someone stationed outside until we catch him."

I turned to Abby. "See? Safest place in town."

I put the kettle on to boil and pulled out the ingredients for a soothing tea. Chamomile, spearmint, and a bit of valerian to help her relax.

"I suppose so."

The kettle boiled, and I poured the water for her.

There was a knock on the open apartment door. Abby jumped. I looked over. "Come in, Kate."

Kate's face had more worry etched on it than I'd ever seen before. "Palmer?" she asked.

"In my room."

Mr. Subramanian left, saying he had just the thing to fix my window.

While Kate and Palmer talked in my room, I made a pot of coffee. I doubted they'd want any, but I had to try.

The two of them left my room. Palmer said, "Let's talk."

"Coffee? Freshly brewed," I said.

Palmer looked like he wanted some, but when Kate said no, he declined as well. Bats! It was going to take a lot more work to get them to trust me.

We sat around the dining table. "I don't think the perp is going to come back tonight. Kate is going to be outside making sure. We don't have much to go on. I've got people asking around, finding out why someone would break in here."

Mr. Subramanian came in, carrying a plywood board and a cordless drill. Mrs. Subramanian, a woman who hardly left her apartment, followed him with a ShopVac.

She took one look at us and said, "You need food. I'll be right back."

Palmer excused himself and went to my room. "I need the large pieces of glass to check for fingerprints," he said.

Kate winced.

"Headache?" I asked.

She nodded slowly. "Yes. It went away for a while, but I can't seem to shake it permanently."

"Is it me?" I asked, hoping she'd see it for the joke I meant.

"Possibly. No one else in town has as many problems as you do."

I looked to Abby, who was not reassured by this comment. She stood up. "I'm going to my room."

Kate rubbed her temples.

"The feverfew you found online not helping your headaches much?" I asked.

"No, it's not. I wish it worked as well as what you gave me at your store."

That didn't surprise me. She should have stopped by and picked up more at the apothecary. "I don't have the same tincture here, but I can make you some tea."

Before she could say anything, I continued. "You can watch me. I promise I'll never give you anything you don't know about again."

She looked doubtful. "Will it work?"

I gave her a quick magical scan to see what she needed. "Yes. Come watch me."

In the kitchen, I took the jar from the tea cabinet and showed it to her. "Just feverfew." I filled a tea infuser and poured the still-hot water in the kettle over the leaves. As the water drew out the healing properties of the feverfew, I infused the tea with my intention for Kate to be headache-free. "Honey?" I asked.

"No. Better not."

I sighed and handed her the mug. "Let the tea steep for a minute and then take the infuser out. You can leave it in the sink."

"You might want to get more sleep, too. Your body can only work well if you treat it well."

She put the infuser in the sink and took a large sip of tea. "I'd like to, but these random, middle-of-the-night calls are killing my sleep schedule."

I frowned. I hated the idea that I was at least a little responsible for her pain. "I'm sorry. I promise I'll try not to have any more emergencies from now on."

Kate looked alarmed. "No, don't feel like that. Promise me, if you have any problems, you'll call." She set her tea down. "I'd take a hundred sleepless nights over you being in danger and not calling."

Her words warmed my heart. "Thank you. Still, I promise I'll try not to have any more emergencies. And if you stop by the apothecary, I'll hook you up with more feverfew. It's the least I can do, since I seem to be the major headache in your life."

She smiled. "I'll consider it."

The lines in her brow were relaxing, a sure sign the tea was starting to work.

Mrs. Subramanian walked into the apartment with a casserole dish. "Rice pudding. It's soothing and will help you get back to sleep. Have some."

She put the dish on the kitchen counter. I lifted the lid and breathed in the cinnamon and nutmeg scent. "It smells delicious. Thank you."

I took two bowls from the dish drainer and put a helping of the creamy rice dish in each. "I'll bring some to Abby."

I knocked on Abby's door. When she didn't answer, I peeked in at her; she was fast asleep.

"She's asleep," I reported when I got to the kitchen. "You should take some rice pudding when you leave," I said to Kate.

The construction sounds coming from my room stopped, and Palmer opened the door. "Your window has been boarded up, and you shouldn't have any more problems with people trying to break in."

"Thank you," I said.

He noticed the mug in Kate's hand and quirked an eyebrow at her.

She gave him a short nod but said nothing.

"Kate and I are going to do a perimeter check, then I'm going to the station, she's staying here. You should be fine for the rest of the night."

I looked at the clock on the oven. 2:37 a.m. I had about seven hours before I had to leave for work, so I'd better make the best of them.

Kate and Palmer left, leaving me with Mr. Subramanian, who was vacuuming my rug. When he turned the vacuum off, I said, "I'd like to ask you a question about Mrs. Thompson."

"In the middle of the night?"

"Well, yes. It should only take a second."

He sighed. "Okay."

"I heard you were raising her rent so high she couldn't afford to live here. Is this true?"

He rubbed his face. "I was raising her rent, but she agreed to the increases."

"I don't understand."

"When she first moved in here, she said she couldn't pay the usual security deposit and last month's rent, so we agreed she would pay some of it each month, until it was all paid off."

That didn't seem bad. Abby and I had saved until we had enough money to pay everything up front. We might have moved sooner, if we knew we could have negotiated a deal with him. "I don't see the problem here."

"The problem was, she never paid the extra. Every month, she paid just the rent and had a sad story about how she'd try harder next month to pay me. I was at the end of my rope. What could I do? I didn't want to ask her to leave, but if word got out I could be taken advantage of, it would be hard to find good renters."

I nodded. "You didn't want her to leave?"

"No. I wanted her to pay what she promised."

"Oh. I heard something different from her friend, Rosemarie. She seemed to think you were raising her rent every month."

He shook his head. "No, that's not what was happening. You should know better than to listen to gossip."

He was probably right, but I had follow every lead in my investigation. "Can I ask you one more question?"

He nodded, even though he looked like he'd rather go back to bed. I didn't blame him.

"Where were you when Mrs. Thompson was murdered?"

"I spend most nights at home, and that's where I was."

"Thanks. Don't let me keep you. Maybe we can both get a little more sleep."

He picked up his tools and vacuum. "Let's hope so. In the morning I'm going to call the alarm company back and have the whole building wired. This building isn't as safe as it used to be, and I won't allow my renters to be in danger."

I smiled. Abby would feel much better when she heard this. "Thank you."

He left and I shut the apartment door. I wondered what other kind of magical protections I could add to the building. I'd have to ask the aunts later on, but only after they'd heard the news about the break-in attempt from someone else.

Chapter 14

One thing I changed about the apothecary was to give myself a day off.

One month of ownership showed me that if I didn't take a day off for myself every week, there was no way I would be able to keep going. In an ideal situation, I'd hire an assistant, but I wasn't ready for that step. And then there was the debate of magical or non-magical assistant. There were benefits to each, and I didn't know which way I wanted to go.

Today was my day off. And what was I doing? Driving up to Sewall with Thea and Agatha. Delia volunteered to stay at the tour company, because they were open seven days a week and probably made more money than I did because of it. The drive was lovely; the mountains of New Hampshire made a great day trip any time of the year.

Sewall wasn't a town just anyone could go to. You needed paranormal DNA to get in. If you weren't a witch, you fell afoul of the wards and seemingly chose not to continue down the road.

We had no problems. Even Agatha, who could read auras, had no difficulty getting in.

When we passed through the wards, the sky suddenly looked different. It was brighter and more colorful, and had a pink tinge you didn't see in the rest of New Hampshire.

Thea drove to the middle of town and parked. Sewall was just about the same as I remembered. But still, it was so different from Portsmouth. The buildings were painted in brighter colors—more like the buildings you'd see in New Mexico. And each building had its own color, regardless of whether it clashed with the surrounding buildings. The trees were all cut into fantasy shapes—have you ever seen an oak tree that looked more like a dragon than a tree? You would in Sewall.

We got out of the car, and Agatha was amazed. "Have you ever been here before?" I asked her.

"No. I had no idea it even existed." She slowly turned around to take in everything on the street. "The entire town is magic?"

I was surprised. We'd come to Sewall for vacations when we were younger, and I assumed every witch family spent time here over the summer. We'd met witch families from all over the country here.

"The whole town. You can't get here if you aren't a witch," I said.

"Your parents didn't take you here for vacation?" Thea asked.

Agatha shook her head. "No vacations for us, we didn't have enough money, and my mother couldn't afford to take time off."

"Well, we're here now. Let's drink it all in," I said.

The florist Thea had parked in front of had displays out on the sidewalk—snapdragons that actually snapped at you if you got too close, and climbing ivy that wound its way around the displays and then back again, as though it was just out for some exercise. I wished I could have some of these in my greenhouse, but their export out of Sewall was prohibited, as you could imagine. I was only able to order dried leaves and flowers.

I took a deep breath, let my guard down a little, and could feel the magic. It felt like going home to Proctor House, where residual magic hung in the air. Here in Sewall, the air was full of magic. I grinned at Agatha. "Can you feel the magic?" I asked.

"I can. I don't like it."

"What do you mean?" I asked.

"Not all of it is good. There's an undercurrent of . . . maliciousness, I think, that I don't like."

I frowned. I wasn't used to Agatha being so coherent or thoughtful. I took a closer look around me. The bright buildings weren't in good repair. Paint was starting to chip, trees had dead branches, and the sidewalk had potholes. The town's upkeep was performed by magic. I let my guard down fully and felt an oily, evil texture swirling around the magic in the town. Agatha was right—there was something wrong with the magic in Sewall.

"Let's go to the potion shop."

Four doors from the florist was Potions by Hester. Grandma told me that if any witch could take care of Agatha, it would be Hester Johnson. We walked in, and I tried not to cough from the green haze in the air. Thea didn't have so much luck and went outside. Each of the walls were covered with jars of dried herbs and animal parts. I shuddered when I saw a jar labeled "Snake Scales." At the back of the store, she had bat wings hanging up, drying just like you'd dry flowers. I'd never been so happy to be a plants-only potion maker.

An old woman looked up from her honest-to-goddess cauldron in the back of the store. I took a good look at her and was astonished. She was the ugliest woman I'd ever seen. Her face was uneven; one side had gone slack, as though she'd had a stroke, and she was covered with warts. I tried not to be a judgmental woman, but in this instance, seeing was believing. A witch only looked this bad if she had performed some bad magic. I hesitated, not sure if I should go in or run out. Grandma had recommended Hester, so I decided I could at least talk to her.

"Can I help you?" the witch asked.

"Hi. I'm looking for Hester Johnson."

"You've found her. And you are?"

"I'm Isabella Proctor. My grandmother, Esther, sent me to talk to you."

Hester cackled. "Esther? I haven't seen her for ages. How is the old bat?"

I smiled. It didn't surprise me that people would think of Grandma as an old bat. She was old and cantankerous. Although—not ugly. "She's well, thank you. She thought you could help my friend Agatha."

Hester stood a little straighter and peered at me. "Were you Trina's apprentice?"

I nodded.

"Sorry for your loss," she said. "Trina was a lovely woman. A little naive, a little simplistic in her worldview. Other than that, she was a good woman."

"Thank you."

She walked around the cauldron and wiped her hands on her dirty apron. "You run her shop now?"

"I do."

"Let me give you some friendly advice, then. You've got to give a little to get a little, you know what I mean?"

I furrowed my brows because I wasn't sure I did.

"You've got to be willing to compromise some to get what you need in life. If that means sometimes you have problems with other people, you smooth them out as best as you can. But keep your priorities intact. Things have changed here, and they'll be changing soon in Portsmouth as well."

This was worrying. Was she trying to warn me? Was this the same problem Trina warned me about in her letter?

"Now, let me see this friend of yours."

Agatha stepped forward. "I'm Agatha."

Hester put her hands on Agatha's head, one on each temple, and closed her eyes. "Hmmm," she murmured.

"You feel better here than you do in Portsmouth?" Hester asked.

"I do. Alice's voice is far away and much easier to ignore right now."

Hester put a hand on Agatha's forehead and stared into her eyes. "Don't blink, how can I see into your soul if you shut me out like that?" Hester asked.

After a long minute of staring into each other's eyes, Hester took her hand off Agatha's forehead and broke eye contact.

"Nothing I can do."

My heart broke. Hester was my last chance. "Are you sure?"

She shook her head. "Maybe a medical doctor can give her something to keep the voice quiet, but there's no way to get it out of her."

"I don't understand. My grandmother told me you were the best potion witch she ever met. I thought you could fix her."

Hester sat on the chair next to her cauldron. "It's a hard lesson to learn as a witch. Sometimes there's no way to fix a problem, and we're stuck with it. Agatha is stuck with Alice's voice. If she wants to stay here in Sewall, she'll be better, at least for a while, but even here the voice will eventually get too strong, and she won't be able to ignore it anymore."

I took Agatha's hand and gave it a squeeze. "Do you want to stay here? Maybe you'll feel better?"

She squeezed my hand back. "No. I'd rather be with my friends, instead of surrounded by strangers."

"How about when we get home, we call my doctor friend?" I asked.

Her eyes welled up with tears. "I guess so, now that I don't have any other hope."

I wanted to cry too. I'd brought her here to give her hope, to show her she could get better. And I'd failed. "Hey, don't say that. We'll try everything we can. I promise I won't let this go unresolved."

She smiled at me. "Thanks. Most people don't take me seriously when I talk about hearing voices."

Hester interrupted our moment. "Isabella, you should spend more time up here with me. I understand your training wasn't quite complete yet. I can teach you a lot that Trina would never consider."

I grimaced. "Thanks, Hester, but I don't know. It's a long drive . . ."

"And I've already scared you off with talk of things changing. No sense in being afraid of the future, when you can prepare for it instead."

"Right. Thanks for your help," I said as I rushed to the door. The last thing I heard as I closed the door behind us was Hester's chilling laugh.

"Was she creepy or what?" Thea asked as we walked down the sidewalk.

"No kidding. You should have heard her."

"I thought you wanted to pick up more ingredients while we were here," Thea said.

"I didn't dare. She frightened me, and I don't trust her."

"Who's next?" Thea asked.

I smiled. "I wanted to visit Grandma's friend Hope."

Before we got to Hope's house, a couple blocks outside of town, we ran into an older man dressed all in black. The black was a contrast to his pale skin and silver hair. He was old, probably older than my mother, but not old enough that he would have gone completely silver naturally. "Excuse me, are you Isabella Proctor?" he asked.

"Yes, I am. Have we met?" I looked at him more closely and realized he had a glamour spell cast around him, keeping us from seeing what he truly looked like. Hester could have used one of those.

He held out a piece of paper to me—the condolence letter I'd written to Mrs. Thompson's son. I briefly wondered if everyone in Sewall had a PO Box in another town, or just the ones who had business outside of the magical community. "Oh, I'm so sorry. I didn't realize who you were."

"Not to worry. I wanted to thank you for this kind note. It's reassuring to know my mother had friends near her in the end. Of course, if she'd have stayed here in Sewall like I asked her to, she'd probably still be alive."

"What makes you say that?"

"I don't know what happens in cities like yours. All I know is that here, we're all safe."

I looked around. Sewall didn't look as safe and clean as it had when I was a kid. "Well, you're welcome for the note. She was a lovely woman, and I'll miss her terribly. You haven't sorted out the details for her funeral yet, have you?"

He looked down at the sidewalk. "Not yet. I need to wait for the police to release her. It will be here, in Sewall. She should be buried among her people. I know who killed her, and I don't want mother's body anywhere near her."

"You know who killed your mother?" I couldn't believe my luck.

"Yes. She was poisoned by Eunice Willoughby."

That seemed impossible. She was a hundred if she was a day. "You mean the witch who lives in the tiny shack over by the river? Have you told the police your theory?"

He scoffed. "No. They'd ignore my idea as soon as they realized how old she was. We know it's the old witches you have to be careful of. Their power doesn't ever decline."

That wasn't exactly true, but if one witch wanted to poison an older one, there were ways to do it.

"I'm sure I'll find a way to prove she did it. But before then, I'd like to come and pick up Jacob," he continued.

"Jacob?" I asked.

"Yes. Mother's cat. I love him, and he's the only piece of mother I have left."

Not much love if he couldn't even get the cat's name right. "His name is Jameson. He's at my apartment. You can call me at the apothecary any day you're in Portsmouth, and we can arrange for you to pick him up."

"That's right, Jameson. I'd like to pick him up tomorrow. If you don't mind, I'm on my way to a meeting," he said, looking anxiously over my shoulder.

"Absolutely. I'm sorry to have kept you."

He brushed past me and joined a startlingly short man who began to yell at him. They were far enough away that I could not hear them.

"He's lying. I wonder what he really wants? Even I know the cat's name," Thea said.

We started walking again, but Agatha didn't keep up with us.

"Agatha, come on!"

"Who was that other man?" Agatha asked.

I turned to look at them. "No idea. Why?"

"He's almost as evil as the man you were talking to."

I hadn't felt Brent was evil. Maybe a bit vindictive, but that was understandable. "Are you feeling okay?"

Agatha shook her head. "Not really."

We followed Grandma's directions to Hope's house. The turquoise-and-pink Victorian was right where she said it would be.

Hope opened the door before we knocked. "Isabella and Thea, so good to see you. Please, come in."

We walked in to her foyer, which held a collection of clocks that were all set to different times. Grandfather clocks, wall clocks, hourglasses, atomic clocks, and even two Apple Watches. "Interesting collection you have here," I commented.

"Thank you, dear." She held her hand out to Agatha. "I'm Hope. Any friend of the Proctors is a friend of mine. Welcome to my home."

Agatha took her hand. "Thank you, Hope."

Again, I was astonished at how well Agatha seemed to be reacting to her surroundings here in Sewall.

"Your grandmother told me you'd be coming for a visit. Why don't we go into the drawing room and have some tea?"

We followed her to the front room on our right. The drawing room was full of Victorian furnishings, tables, and even a piano. "Please, sit. I'll get the tea."

She waved her hand and a door opened, allowing a tray carrying a teapot, lemon, sugar, and milk to waft its way to the low table we were sitting around. A three-tiered serving piece followed, full of sandwiches, scones, and desserts.

"This looks so lovely," I said. "You didn't need to go to so much trouble for us."

Hope began to pour tea. "Lemon chamomile today, ladies."

We spent a few minutes preparing our tea and choosing food before we got down to business.

"I asked your grandmother to make sure you stopped by, because I have important information you need to know. First, how close were you to Mrs. Thompson?"

I frowned. "Not really close, but we talked several times a week. She invited me over, and we talked or played cards. I also watched her cat, Jameson, when she left town. I guess I'd say we were close for neighbors, but she wasn't ever going to be my best friend, if that's what you mean."

Hope nodded. "I suppose that's to be expected, given the large gap between your ages. Who has the cat now?"

"I do. When I found her, he bolted out of her apartment and waited at my door until I let him in. He's barely let me out of his sight since then. He comes with me to work, and honestly, I'm surprised he let me come here without making a big stink about my leaving the apartment."

"Interesting. Have you noticed anything . . . different about him?"

I pursed my lips. "I don't think so, other than he doesn't want me to go anywhere without him."

"You may notice something in the future."

"Like what?"

"I'd rather not speculate right now. The reason I wanted you here is to talk about the amulet—the Bishop amulet."

She said "Bishop amulet" with such a tone of voice that it was obvious she thought I knew what she was talking about. Unfortunately, I had no clue.

When I didn't say anything, she continued. "And this is the problem with raising young witches outside their community. You are missing out on valuable information that needs to be passed down."

"Maybe you could tell us about the Bishop amulet?" Thea asked.

"It looks like I'm going to have to, now, aren't I?" She sat back and closed her eyes. When she opened them, she started talking quickly. "The Bishop amulet is one of the seven protective charms that keep witches safe in New Hampshire. Each has a guardian, who is tasked with using it to protect witches if they are in danger. Beatrice was its last guardian."

I nodded. "And you want me to find the amulet and bring it to you?"

"Oh, goddess, no! I'm far too old to start carrying an amulet."

"But Mrs. Thompson was old."

"She wasn't when she was first chosen to carry it."

Oh. Broomsticks! I knew where this was going.

"She was in Portsmouth looking for a new guardian. She thought you might be it."

"I don't have the amulet, though. I suppose I can search her apartment, but wouldn't the person who killed her have already found it?"

"No. The well-being of Sewall is tied to the amulet. Did you notice the dead limbs, peeling paint and general disrepair when you got here? This is how I know the amulet hasn't got a new owner. If a good owner had it, the town would be back to its former self. If a bad person had it, the town would have lost all its protection by now."

She leaned closer to me and grabbed my hand. "You need to find the amulet and claim it as yours."

"What if she didn't think I was the right person for it?"

"We don't have a choice now. It has to be yours."

I pulled my hand out from hers. I wasn't sure I wanted this responsibility. I definitely didn't feel like I was ready for it. Nothing we'd talked about seemed designed to prepare me for the responsibility of keeping witches in New Hampshire safe.

"Can't I just bring it back to town and let someone else take it?"

Hope shook her head. "One thing Beatrice knew was that no one in town should have the amulet. She wouldn't have left if there was anyone here to pass it on to. She felt drawn to Portsmouth, and to you in particular. You were her best choice."

Batwings. "How about my mother?"

"I understand your reluctance, but if you are the next owner, everything will make sense to you, once you find it. Magic doesn't leave these things to chance. If you want, once you find it, come see me and we can talk more. I'll help you find your way through what you need to do."

I frowned. "Okay. I guess that will help."

Agatha stood up. "We need to get going. We've got to find this amulet before anyone else does."

I turned to Agatha. Why was she so insistent? "Do you know something I don't?"

She bit her lip and turned away. "Not really. I have a feeling other people are looking for it, and they're getting close."

"Agatha, what aren't you telling me?"

"Nothing important. Let's go."

Thea stood up. "I think Agatha is right."

"We don't even know what the amulet looks like," I protested.

"Emerald in a gold setting. About as big as a quail's egg. You could mistake it for a non-magical piece of jewelry if you didn't know better," said Hope.

"Okay then, I guess we'll go."

Once we left the house, Agatha practically pushed us down the street until we got to our car. "Drive fast," she told Thea.

Chapter 15

The drive home from Sewall was long, and I spent more time thinking about the heavy responsibility Mrs. Thompson may have wanted to give me. I was an average, ordinary witch with no special talents. It seemed like a mistake to put the safety, even one-seventh of the safety, of New Hampshire witches in my inexperienced hands.

I shouldn't say "may have," because once Hope brought up the amulet, I knew Mrs. T. had intended for me to take it; she was taking her time and easing me in slowly. But why? Why did she think I was up for the challenge? Maybe if I could find the witches who were holding the other six . . . I wasn't even sure what else they were holding. Were they holding other amulets? A variety of objects?

Being a witch just got a lot more complicated.

Agatha slept the entire ride home, and Thea, seeing I wanted to think, left me alone.

We drove straight to my apartment, because I wanted their help searching for the amulet. The sky turned gray once we left Sewall, and the scenery passed in a blur as I contemplated the completely different path my future was taking.

The first thing I noticed when we got home was Mrs. T.'s apartment was no longer guarded. Did this mean the investigation was over, and Palmer had caught her killer? I didn't think so. It would take more than he had to catch a witch. We went straight in and the apartment was just as I saw it last. Tidy, organized, but soulless now, with no occupant.

"How are we going to find the amulet?" Thea asked.

"I was thinking about that. I hoped I'd feel some sort of connection to it, but . . ." I closed my eyes and used my senses to feel around the apartment. "So far, nothing."

"I guess we ought to try the obvious places, like her jewelry box, just in case," Thea said.

Agatha walked out of the living room and into the kitchen. "I don't think it's here. I mean, if it were here, then whoever killed her would have taken it."

She had a good point.

"I'm going to clean out the kitchen instead. There's no need for her food to go bad, right?" Agatha asked.

This seemed sensible, and even better, sensible for Agatha. Maybe the effects she'd felt in Sewall would last now that we were back in Portsmouth.

"I'll take the office," Thea said.

I took the bedroom. The drapes were still closed, making it too dark to see anything. I turned on the light and opened the drapes to let in the last of the evening sunlight. Her open jewelry box rested atop her bureau. I looked inside, but there was no amulet. In fact, she had very little jewelry there at all. A pearl ring, a pair of topaz earrings, and a gold band. Perhaps most of her jewelry had been stolen already. Surely a woman doesn't need such a large box to hold so little. The only other objects on the bureau were a silver vanity set of brush, comb, and mirror.

I looked through her drawers. They were also mostly empty. Were most of her clothes in her laundry hamper, or did she have very little to her name? Her closet held two dresses, two pairs of shoes, one pair of boots, and one winter coat.

A horrible thought occurred to me. What if she'd been selling her things to pay the rent? Poor Mrs. T.! If I'd known she had so little, I would never have charged her full price for Jameson's kidney tonic.

At any rate, I found no amulet in the drawers, pockets of her clothing, or shoes. Her nightstand had one book on it, *A Mother's Reckoning*, and nothing in the drawer. I got down on my hands and knees and looked under the bed.

Nothing.

Not even dust bunnies.

Desperate to find something, I ran my hands along the curtains, investigated the curtain rods, and even squished her pillows, feeling for anything hard.

As a last-ditch attempt, I lifted her mattress, even though I wasn't fond of the idea of touching the place she'd died. There was nothing underneath it.

I left, frustrated, and checked on Agatha. "How's it going?" I asked.

"Not bad. I've got the refrigerator emptied out. She wouldn't mind if I didn't save all reusable plastic containers, would she?"

I stared into Agatha's eyes. A little of the cloudy uncertainty she usually had was creeping back in. "She's dead, Agatha. She doesn't need plastic containers."

She looked sheepish. "I guess you're right."

"Keep up the good work. I'm going to check on Thea," I said.

On the office floor, Thea had made neat piles of everything that had been on or in Mrs. Thompson's desk. "Find anything good?" I asked.

"No amulet, but she owed a lot of people money. She had an entire drawer devoted to overdue bills."

Had she come to Portsmouth with nothing to live on? How had she expected to survive, if she had no money to support herself?

"I'm going to start in on the living room," I said, discouraged that my friend was living so meager a life, and I never even noticed. At the very least, Abby and I could have brought her day-old pastry from The Fancy Tart.

The living room was simple to investigate. One couch, two chairs, a small table, a lamp and a window. Nothing held any surprises.

Thea joined Agatha and me as I finished up. "It's not here, is it?"

I shook my head. "Is there anything you can do?"

"Like what?" Thea asked.

"Can you use one piece of her jewelry to locate another?"

"I don't think psychometry works that way, but I can give it a try."

I stepped into the bedroom to retrieve Mrs. T.'s few pieces of jewelry. I handed them to Thea, but she handed them back. "One at a time is best."

I handed her the gold band. Thea closed her eyes. "All I see here is Mrs. T. and her husband at different times of their life together."

"I don't think that's going to get us anywhere."

I handed her the topaz earrings. "Oh, these were a gift from her son, when he was much younger. I can see the last time she wore them, and they made her sad. The thought of her son made her sad. She wished he had gotten married, had kids and settled down. He never did, and so she never had the grandchildren she wanted."

I handed her the last piece of jewelry, the pearl ring. "Oooh," Thea crooned. "This was given to her by another man."

"Really? Who?"

"I don't know. She loved him, even though they never married."

How sad. "That sounds like a heartbreaking story, probably not amulet-related, though."

Thea shook her head. "You should put these back. I'm sure her son would want them."

"Agatha, did you find anything?" I asked.

She giggled. "I did! I found this." She brandished a Cadbury egg. "Do you know how hard it is to get these when it's not Easter?"

Agatha wasn't wrong, but a quick look at her revealed she'd quickly gone straight back to her usual self. "Agatha, how are you feeling?"

"I'm good. Alice is getting bored and wants to go."

My heart cracked a bit for her. "In a minute. I want to ask you a question first. Come sit on the couch with me."

We sat and I took her hand. "I want you to remember how you felt when we were in Sewall. Can you do that?"

She nodded. "I liked it there. Alice was quiet, and just before we left, I was the only one in my head. It was spooky, and I wondered where she went."

"Would you like to go back? Do you want to feel that way all the time?"

Agatha frowned. "I'd miss my friends. I'd miss you, and I'd even miss Alice, at least some of the time."

My heart broke. Shattered for her. "I think there's something in Sewall that helps you, something you can't get here in Portsmouth, and if you stayed there, you'd have a healthier mind. I want to take you back next week to see if you feel good again there. Just as soon as we find who killed Mrs. Thompson, we'll go. Okay?"

"If that's what you want, Isabella, sure. We can do that."

I took a deep breath and tried to keep tears out of my eyes. "I'm going to my apartment. It's been a long day, and I need to relax and think about what to do next."

"I'll bring Agatha home," Thea volunteered.

Back in my apartment, Jameson rushed to meet me at the door. I bent down to pet him. "Wow, if you're going to be like this when I get home, I should leave you here more often."

He meowed at me and walked into the bathroom. I sat on the couch, happy Abby wasn't home. I didn't want to make up an explanation about how my day went that wouldn't include Sewall, a magic amulet, or a customer whose illness got better in a town I couldn't even talk about.

Jameson meowed from the bathroom, but I ignored him.

He jumped up on me and purred. I heard my name off in the distance, but there was no one here. I looked at Jameson, and he just meowed.

"I must be more exhausted than I thought I was. I'm hearing things."

Jameson walked into the bathroom, and this time, he howled.

"All right, all right. I'm coming. I can't imagine what's so important that you want me to come in here."

There was nothing wrong with the bathroom. The litter box didn't need to be emptied out, everything was tidy and I didn't see any evidence of mice or other animals that would have him howl. "What's wrong?" I asked.

He howled again, but didn't give me any clues. Maybe he needed food.

I walked into the kitchen and saw his food and water were empty. "Poor little guy, no wonder you're howling. You're hungry." I filled his water and food bowls, and he left the bathroom to eat.

Chapter 16

I spent the rest of the night thinking. What else could I do? I felt like I was running out of options.

I still hadn't given up on Agatha, though. Seeing her progress in Sewall gave me hope that there was a cure out there somewhere.

This morning, though, Thea, Delia, and I were going to see Eunice Willoughby. I wanted to see if the information Brent had given us yesterday had any truth. I couldn't imagine she could cause much trouble, because she was even older than Grandma—but then again, I didn't see Grandma slowing down anytime soon.

We decided to go before work. Investigating murder was tough when you had to squeeze it into nonwork hours. Thea and Delia were waiting in my parking lot when I made my way out with three travel mugs of morganmuffel tea. This was the best tea for starting a morning earlier than you wanted to—less caffeine than coffee, with ten times more alertness. I was still testing it, and planned to offer it later this year at the apothecary.

Eunice's house was a run-down cottage with a small dock on the Piscataqua River, which formed part of the border between New Hampshire and Maine. The tiny yard had front and side gardens. The front was full of flowers, and the side had raised beds of what looked like vegetables. If Eunice took care of these herself, she would have had plenty of energy to kill Mrs. Thompson. Her curtains were all drawn, and I began to feel guilty for coming so early in the morning.

We opened her gate and strode up to the front door. I knocked, but there was no answer. I frowned. You'd think a witch would have some sort of ward set on her gate to let her know when people were there. I looked around at her front garden. Roses were blooming, daylilies were starting to sprout up, and the rhododendron was in full bloom.

Thea knocked on the door. Still no answer.

"Maybe she's still sleeping? We should come back later," Delia said.

I shook my head. "Let's check out back."

We walked to the side of her house, and I scanned her raised garden beds. The first was tomatoes and garlic. The plants were thriving and healthy. She must have spent a lot of time learning gardening craft.

Delia stifled a scream and pointed to another bed. Agatha lay there, unmoving.

We ran to Agatha, and I checked for her pulse, even though the finger marks around her neck told me not to bother. She was dead.

Delia put her hand on mine and slowly pulled me away from Agatha. "She's gone."

I didn't think I could call Palmer to tell him I'd found another dead person. On the other hand, I couldn't leave Agatha here.

"What's going on here?" a woman called from the backyard.

"Mrs. Willoughby? Stay there," Thea said.

Like any old witch worth her salt, she ignored the command and came to see what we were staring at. "Oh no, not again. I can't have this."

And Agatha's body disappeared.

I was dumbfounded. What did she do? Where did she send Agatha? And what did she mean when she said "not again"? "Hey! You can't do that," I protested.

"Bring her back!" Thea demanded.

Eunice looked at us with squinty eyes. "Who are you, and what do you want, bothering an old woman this early in the morning?"

"Mrs. Willoughby, did you kill Agatha?" Thea asked.

"Don't be an out-and-out fool, girl. I was going to ask you the same thing. I found you standing over her corpse."

"On your property," Thea shot back.

"Now none of us can get in trouble. No body, no crime. So why don't you girls go back to whatever high school you came from and leave me alone."

High school? Now that was just insulting.

"We seem to have gotten off on the wrong foot," Delia said as she stepped in front of Thea. It looked to me like she was trying to shield our cousin from whatever damage Eunice could cause.

"My name is Delia Proctor. Perhaps you know my family?"

Eunice squinted at Delia. "You're Essie's what? Granddaughter?"

Delia smiled. "Yes. And these are my cousins."

Eunice relaxed as she examined us more thoroughly. "Why didn't you say so at the beginning? No more of this "Mrs. Willoughby" nonsense, you call me Eunice. Let's go inside and sit."

Not a good plan. First, she had been accused of killing Mrs. Thompson, and then when we showed up, we found a second dead body. Maybe it wasn't such a good idea to be here without an older, more experienced witch to back us up. Of course, that would involve the family, and I didn't want to tell the aunts or, goddess forbid, Grandma, what had been going on in my life this week. Can you imagine what they would do? I could, and I was hoping to get away without telling them anything.

"I'd rather stay here, if you don't mind," I said.

"Can you bring our friend Agatha back?" Delia asked quietly.

"Why would I want to do that? No evidence, no conviction. I don't think any of us want to get in trouble with the law, do we?"

I'm not sure she meant this to sound like a threat, but I shivered anyway.

"Isabella has worked with the police in the past, and they're more likely to trust her."

Lisa Bouchard

"Let's not worry about where Agatha is right now," Thea said. "We're here to talk about Beatrice Thompson."

At the name of Mrs. Thompson, the wind seemed to go out of Mrs. Willoughby's sails. "She was a good woman and an uncommonly fine witch. I can't believe she's gone."

"Yes, right. We're all sad about her passing. But my question for you is, did you kill her?" Thea asked.

"Why would I want to kill her?" Eunice asked.

"I don't know . . . maybe for the amulet she had?" Delia blurted out.

Bats! Thea must have told Delia everything that happened yesterday. I didn't specifically say we shouldn't mention the amulet. I guess I should have.

"What amulet?" Eunice asked.

"The Bishop amulet. The one she was here to give to Isabella."

And that was it. The entire story was out. Delia was going to have to stop trusting people so much, if we were going to get anywhere in our investigations.

Eunice stared at me, eyes widening. "You?"

I nodded. "I didn't know until yesterday when I went to Sewall. Hope told us."

"Mrs. Thompson wasn't talking to any other young witches," Thea said.

"We searched her apartment, but couldn't find it," I said.

Eunice frowned. "That's problematic."

"We think she may have been killed for it."

"By me? That doesn't make any sense, girl. If she was too old for it, and was passing it on, why on earth would I want it? I'm much older than she was."

She was right. That didn't make a lot of sense.

"Maybe you didn't want it for yourself, maybe you wanted to pass it down to someone else, someone you could control," Thea said.

"Someone I could control?" Eunice parroted back. "No. If I wanted anything to do with the politics of Sewall, I'd have stayed there. All I want is to tend my gardens, although lettuce looks like it's off the menu for the summer, and grow old in peace."

"So where were you four nights ago when Beatrice was murdered?" I asked.

"Aha! Finally, the alibi question. I was here, alone. No one to verify, not even a familiar."

"Not as helpful as you might think—" Delia began.

"Of course it's not helpful. But it's all I've got."

"And how about last night and earlier this morning? Did you hear anything or see anyone?" I asked.

Eunice shook her head. "Not a peep. Of course, that doesn't mean anything. You saw how easy it is to silently move a dead body from one place to another."

"Why didn't you call the police when you first saw her, when you came outside earlier?"

"I haven't even made it out here to the side yard yet. I was working behind the house when you got here."

I frowned. I still hadn't gotten the hang of getting people's alibis. No one ever wanted to tell you where they really were or what they were really doing. I looked at the bed of lettuce Agatha had been resting on. Entangled in some of the leaves was a clump of gray hair. I teased one strand from the edge and held it up. "Is this your hair?" I asked.

Eunice laughed. She pulled the hair sticks that were holding her large bun in place and shook her hair out. "I haven't cut my hair, other than a trim, for over twenty years. I hardly think such a short strand came from me."

She was right. Her wavy white hair fell past her knees, and the hair in my hand was only a couple inches long.

"Fine. Then if you didn't kill her, why did you get rid of the body so quickly? That seems like the action of a guilty person," Thea said.

I wasn't so sure about that. I knew from experience being found near too many dead bodies was likely to give the police ideas. Ideas that landed you in an interrogation room at best, in jail at worst.

"Can we bring her back? I'd like to take another look at her for clues. And it's better if we call the police rather than making them come to us."

"Why would the police come to you?" Eunice asked.

"Thea and I spent the day with Agatha yesterday, in Sewall. That's bound to come out sooner or later."

"Not the Sewall part, though," Delia said.

"Spending the day with her will be enough for Palmer to take a good look at me," I said.

"Fine," Eunice said. "Step away from the planter. It's hard work to do this, and my aim might be off a little."

Agatha popped into view, but Eunice was right. Her aim was off, and Agatha was half in, half out of the lettuce bed. "Should we move her?" I asked.

Thea and Delia shrugged their shoulders.

I looked to Eunice, but she didn't seem to care. "She wasn't killed here, so whether she's in exactly the right position doesn't matter."

"Why do you think she was killed somewhere else?" I asked.

Eunice rolled her eyes. "Look at the lettuce. Most of it is untouched. A person doesn't give up without a fight when she's being strangled like this. She claws around, looking for a weapon, for anything to save her life. At least until she blacks out."

Poor Agatha! I had a quick flash of her, confused and alone, staring into the eyes of her killer. He was the last thing she saw in life, and that didn't seem fair. I brushed away the tear that had fallen on my cheek. "Horrible," was all I could whisper.

Last night I was sure I could find a way to care for Agatha. A way to get her mind focused and, at the very least, to quiet the voice of Alice in her head. I imagined I could find how Sewall had healed her mind and then, somehow, transport it to Portsmouth. Guilt washed through me. If I hadn't put her off, telling her that I would take care of her after I found Mrs. Thompson's killer, she might still be alive today. We would have worked well into the night, and I could have protected her when her murderer came calling.

"Isabella? Are you okay?" I heard Delia as though from a distance. Suddenly her arms were around me, and I sank into her support.

"Easy there," she said. "What's wrong?"

"It's my fault. I should have saved her."

Chapter 17

We need to get help," Thea said.

I nodded. We were definitely outside the realm of things we could handle for ourselves. "Eunice, after we leave, I want you to call the police and tell them you found a body in your garden. You don't need to mention us though."

She didn't look like she liked the idea, even though she agreed. "I suppose so. They're not going to put an old woman like me in jail, are they?"

We walked to the car and drove the few blocks to Proctor House.

"I hate that we're going to have to come clean about all the investigating we've been doing. The aunts are not going to be happy with us," Thea said.

"Do we need to tell them everything?" I asked.

Thea and Delia looked at me. I shrank back into my seat. "Okay, yes. We do. It's just that if we skipped a few things, maybe it wouldn't look so bad?"

"And what, exactly, would you omit?" Thea asked.

I thought for a moment. "Nothing. It's all related in one way or another."

"Anyone know a charm spell to keep them from getting too mad?" Delia asked.

I chuckled. We'd never found one that worked on the aunts, even after years of trying.

We walked into the kitchen, ready to face the music.

Aunt Nadia turned to us and said, "Oh, girls. You're in time for breakfast. Take these scones into the dining room."

Scones? Dining room? Breakfast wasn't usually a family meal, and we hardly ever ate more than a quick muffin as we walked out the door. I took the plate from her and walked into the dining room, to see my mother, Aunt Lily, and Grandma sitting in silent anticipation.

The atmosphere in the blue dining room was serious. Even the wall sconces seemed to be sending out less light.

"It's about time you girls came to talk to us," Grandma said.

With nothing to lose, I went for the innocent approach. "What do you mean?"

My mother looked at me, her lips pressed together so tightly they were almost white. "Do you honestly think we don't know what's happening in your lives? Do you think we don't hear the gossip in town? And do you really think you can spend a day in Sewall and not have half the town calling us to ask what's going on?"

"I guess not," I said dejectedly. "Scone?"

I set the plate on the table and took a seat. Delia and Thea sat next to me.

Aunt Nadia came in with a pot of coffee and poured us each a mug.

"Let's get this family meeting started. I don't have all day to hang around here," Grandma said.

Since her brush with illness a few months ago, she'd gotten a new energy and wanted to make sure she spent her days doing things, not sitting around "like an old woman," she said.

"I think we'd like to hear from Isabella. She seems to be the ringleader here," my mother said.

"You're right. We were in Sewall yesterday, but Grandma knew that, because she told us to go talk to Hope."

Grandma scowled. "You didn't have to rat me out, did you?"

"Why did you tell them to see Hope?" my mother asked.

"Hope called me. She said she needed to talk to the girls right away. All I did was relay the message."

"I suppose the most important thing to say is that we found Agatha, dead, at Eunice Willoughby's this morning," I said.

"Poor child, she never stood a chance in life. How did she kill herself?" Aunt Nadia asked.

"She didn't. It looked to me like she was strangled."

"And what did the police say?"

"We told Eunice to call them after we left," Delia said.

"You left the scene of a crime? Palmer is going to be angry with you," Aunt Lily said.

"I'd like to know what you were doing in Sewall," Aunt Nadia said.

"It all started with Agatha. There's nothing else I can do to help her, and she won't go see a doctor. I told her we could go and see Hester, who might know more than I did. Thea, Agatha, and I went up there yesterday. The amazing thing was, in Sewall, Agatha seemed almost normal. She was definitely more rational, and she said the voice in her head was farther away. Anyway, Hester couldn't help us. We ran into Brent Thompson on our way to see Hope, and he says he wants Jameson. I guess he'll be coming down to pick him up sometime today."

"Why is he telling you he wants the cat?" Grandma asked.

"Because Jameson is staying in my apartment. I've gotten fond of him, and I don't want to give him up. I suppose I have to, though."

Aunt Nadia stared at me. "How, exactly, did the cat come to stay with you?"

"When I found Mrs. Thompson, he ran to my door and waited for me there when I went in to look for her."

"You didn't force him or carry him into your apartment?"

I shook my head. "He walked in on his own four paws."

Aunt Nadia looked to her sisters. "Do you think?"

"We can work that out later. Right now, we need to find out what else the girls haven't told us," my mother said.

I took a deep breath. "Did you hear about the break-in at my apartment last night?" I asked.

I didn't look at my mother—I didn't want to see how mad she was.

"I knew. I felt my wards being tested," Aunt Lily said.

"Your wards? The guy tried to break in through my bedroom window. I thought you only put wards on the door."

"When you first moved in, yes. But after Abby was kidnapped, the six of us spent a week putting wards on all your windows as well," Aunt Nadia said.

It all made sense now. That's why he couldn't put his hand through the opening. The combined work of the rest of my family would be almost impossible for anyone to get through. I'd been waiting for him to breach my ward and decide he needed to go somewhere else. He never had the chance, because the family's ward was layered over mine. "He broke the window, but couldn't put his hand through the hole in the glass. Now the entire window is covered by a sheet of plywood. I imagine my landlord will replace the glass soon, if he hasn't already."

I took a sip of my coffee. "I never saw you out there."

My mother leaned back in her chair. "We worked in shifts, but even so, it would have alarmed the neighbors to see someone watching the building for a week, so we used a simple invisibility spell."

"Nothing was taken?" Aunt Nadia asked.

I shook my head. "Abby is upset again, though. Even with the new alarm system."

"What did Hope have to say?" Grandma asked.

"Apparently, Mrs. Thompson had the Bishop amulet, and she was here to pass it on to me."

"Don't accept it," my mother blurted out. "You're under no obligation to. Let someone else carry the burden."

"Now, Michelle," Aunt Nadia soothed, "you know the amulets don't work that way."

"She's too young. There's no way she ought to have that kind of responsibility."

"So you know all about being a guardian and the other six pieces keeping witches safe? Why didn't you ever teach us?"

The aunts all looked to Grandma. "The Proctor family has always declined to carry any of the protective amulets. It's too much of a burden, and we didn't want to put future generations through it."

"The amulets pass down in families?"

"Usually. Beatrice didn't think her son should have it. That's why she had to come down here. No one in Sewall was good enough."

Not good enough? "What do you mean?" I asked.

"When Sewall was set up, it was for protection, but also for study. The witches of the time were having their own sort of renaissance. New, useful spells and potions were being developed at a rapid speed, and the town's inhabitants were focused on helping others.

"Now, the best of them just want to live separately, and the worst of them, they want to show their power and start using it on non-witches."

"Okay, I can see why she didn't think the amulet should go to anyone up there, I just don't see why she would pick me."

Grandma shook her head. "I couldn't tell you."

Couldn't or wouldn't? The only thing I knew was she wouldn't change her mind about telling me.

"I hate to interrupt the history lesson, but we need to make a plan. Someone is in town, killing witches. We're being specifically targeted," Aunt Lily said.

I knew the first thing anyone was going to say was I needed to move home.

"I think Delia and I should go stay with Isabella. At least until we catch the murderer," said Thea.

A chorus of "no" and "absolutely not" filled the dining room.

"We're safer in numbers, and maybe we can catch him if he tries to break in again. Whoever it is can't be too strong, magically speaking, or he would have noticed the wards and tried to break them first."

"Stupid people can kill as easily as smart people," my mother said. "It's best for Isabella to give up the apartment permanently and move home."

I smiled at Thea as a thanks for trying. We both knew her idea wouldn't work. "We've been through this enough already. I'm not moving."

The doorbell for the front door rang. I looked at my watch. Who would be coming to the house at nine in the morning?

Aunt Lily answered the door, and when she returned, Palmer was with her.

"Isabella, you need to come down to the station to answer some questions about the death of Agatha Hubert."

Chapter 18

Was it wrong the first thing I thought was, "Aha! That's her last name"?

"Please stand up," Palmer said.

I stood and the rest of the women around the table began to all talk at once.

"You know I didn't kill her, right?"

"Your fingerprint was on her necklace charm."

I pursed my lips. "I spent the day with her yesterday, so it makes sense. Shouldn't you question me first, get my alibi? You know what the chief is going to say."

"I won't need to use the cuffs on you, will I?"

Cuffs? Weren't they only for people who were arrested? "No. You don't need to worry about me running away from you. I'll answer your questions because I want to find out who killed Agatha and Mrs. Thompson at least as much as you do."

"You can question her here," my mother said.

"I'd rather not have the interference, if it's all the same to you," Palmer said.

My mother scowled at him. "Fine. I'll call my lawyer, and he will meet you at the station."

I rolled my eyes. "That's not necessary. He just wants to ask me questions—I've survived his questioning before, so I'm sure I'll be fine now. I'll call you when I get out, okay?"

I could see the effort it took her, but she said, "Okay. You do what you think is best."

Out in the car, he had me sit in the back seat. That's when I knew I was in more trouble than usual. "Tell me, why are you bringing me in?"

"I'd rather talk once we get to the station."

"Okay, then . . . so how are you?"

"Isabella," he snapped, "this isn't a social call. You might be in a lot of trouble right now, and chitchat isn't going to get you out of it."

Wow, what was bothering him today? I'd find out during the interrogation, I supposed. We spent the rest of the drive in silence, and I noticed he spent more time than I expected looking at me through the rearview mirror. He didn't look happy, either.

He pulled into the rear parking lot of the station, and I tried to open my door, forgetting that it only worked from the outside. Great. I had to wait for him to let me out.

He opened my door and held his hand out to help me out of the car. I reached out and took his, hoping it was a gesture of friendliness, but it wasn't. He did that weird cop thing where he switched his hold to my elbow and propelled me into the station. I'd already told him I would cooperate. Why did he think I would change my mind?

We walked to the same interrogation room I'd been in a few months before and sat down. "Same room, brings back some unpleasant memories," I said.

Was the chief was behind the one-way mirror? I tried to probe the area but couldn't feel anyone there. The fluorescent light buzzed, and I wondered if they didn't replace the light on purpose.

Palmer sat in front of me, on the other side of the table. "Before we begin, I want to say how disappointed I am in you. I thought we'd worked things out the morning you found Mrs. Thompson. I thought you were going to keep your nose out of police business and stay away from dead bodies."

I flashed a small smile at him. "To be fair, I don't go looking for bodies, they just sort of show up in my path. Don't you think I'd rather have Mrs. Thompson alive? Rather have Agatha still living?"

"I guess that all depends on your relationship with each of them."

He pressed record and started the official interrogation. "I'd like to start by asking you how long you've known Agatha Hubert and what your relationship with her was."

Starting with the easy questions? Fine by me. "Agatha was a customer of mine. She came to the apothecary—the apothecary I should be opening right now—at least once a week. I've known her since I started there as Trina's apprentice, so a little more than a year."

"Did you ever see her outside the apothecary?"

"I had, occasionally, served her when I still worked at The Fancy Tart, and sometimes she stopped me on the street to chat."

"Would you say you were friends?"

I pursed my lips. "No. Not really. I pitied her too much to be a real friend to her."

"Why?"

"She had a mental illness that kept her from being a fully functional member of society." And for that, I really did feel sorry for her. To say she wasn't my friend? I'm not sure that was true. I cared about her well-being, I didn't allow people to mock her, and I missed her if I didn't see her regularly. I guess we were friends.

He quirked an eyebrow at me.

"She heard voices. Specifically, one voice named Alice who told her what to do and made her life miserable."

"Is that what she saw you for? A treatment?"

I nodded. "Yes. It had become apparent I couldn't help her more than I already was. I tried to talk her into seeing a doctor, but she didn't want to. She didn't trust them."

"What did you treat her with?"

"I made her a tincture with ashwagandha and chamomile. It helped quiet the voice a little bit, so at least she could sleep most nights."

"How did your fingerprint come to be on her necklace?"

"We spent some of the day together yesterday. It was my day off."

"You spent your day off with a woman who you've already said wasn't your friend? That seems strange."

Oh spells! I couldn't explain what we were doing yesterday.

"Thea and I took a drive up to the mountains yesterday, and I asked Agatha if she wanted to come with us. Sometimes, a change of scenery is relaxing, and I thought she could use the trip."

"Again, even though she wasn't your friend?"

"Yes. But I think maybe we were friends, at least a little bit. She can't hold down a job in her condition, so she has basically nothing. She never leaves town, never sees anything different, and I thought it might make her happy." I looked at him sternly. "I'm nice, even to people who aren't my friends."

"Any witnesses to your trip yesterday other than your cousin?"

I shook my head. "No. I doubt the cashier at the gas station we filled up at on the drive home would remember us, and we didn't stop anywhere else."

"No lunch?" he asked.

"No. I guess we weren't hungry."

"Really? No snacks, nothing?"

"It's tough to keep this girlish figure," I said. There was no way I could tell him about stopping for tea at Hope's.

Palmer stood and opened the door to the interrogation room after we heard a knock. A clerk was waiting for him outside with a folder. "Thanks," he told the clerk as he shut the door.

Back at the table, he displayed a series of photos for me to look at. "Can you explain these?"

I was surprised to see they were photos of me. Me walking down the street, me in my apartment taken through a window, me at work. None of the photos had been taken at close range, but they were close enough to be worrying. "I don't know. Who took these?"

"We found them at Agatha's apartment. She had a lot more than this—all of you, or you and other members of your family."

I shuddered. "Creepy."

"Did you ever get the feeling she was stalking you?"

That startled me. "No. Never. I don't think she was capable of stalking."

"Then how do you explain her journal entries that refer to you as her best friend? She details meeting you for breakfast at the Fancy Tart many times, and even recalls some of your conversations."

"She . . . she what? I've never made a breakfast date with her in my life." I was starting to get worried. "Honestly, we were just acquaintances, and she was a customer of mine."

Palmer looked into my eyes. "Isabella. If you felt threatened, or like you were in any danger from her, now is the time to tell me. If there were mitigating circumstances, that can go a long way in your defense."

"I never . . . did I . . . what?"

"Take a minute and relax. It's important to think about your next moves carefully."

My next moves? All I could think of was getting out of there—running until my problems couldn't find me anymore.

"Agatha never threatened me. At no time did I think she'd ever hurt anyone except maybe herself." I stood up. "And now, I'm done answering your questions. If you need to speak to me again, you can contact my lawyer."

Palmer smiled. "Sure. Name?"

"I don't know. Whoever my mother was going to call, I guess."

"Just one more second, please. There's something going on with your family. I don't know what it is, but I'm going to figure it out. When I do, you'd better hope I don't find anything illegal."

"Great. Whatever."

I walked to the door, but he beat me to it. "Isabella Proctor, I'm placing you under arrest for the murder of Agatha Hubert." I could barely focus as he read me my Miranda rights, led me back to the table and sat me down.

"I hope you appreciate the trouble you're in now and that you decide to fully cooperate. Tell me about the necklace."

"I already explained the fingerprint. I looked at her necklace yesterday."

"Where were you last night between eleven o'clock and two in the morning?"

"I was in my apartment, asleep."

"Can anyone vouch for you?"

"Abby can."

He frowned. "You two don't share a room. You could have waited until she fell asleep and then sneaked out."

"I suppose I could have, but I wouldn't. Sheesh, Palmer! You know me, you know I'm not a murderer. I'm an herbalist, I help people, not kill them."

"Unfortunately for you, we have another witness who said Agatha's body showed up when you did this morning."

Eunice! I can't believe she said that. I suppose she might think it was true, but she told us she hadn't even been in her side yard until we got there. How would she know if Agatha had been there before we got there?

Chapter 19

Of all the indignities, Palmer booked me and locked me in a holding cell. Then he left me alone for what seemed like hours.

The longer I waited, the more I was sure I was going to miss meeting Brent to turn over Jameson. The apothecary was closed and I doubted Abby would be home in the middle of the day. I'd have to get in touch with him and reschedule.

On the other hand, I wasn't sad about not getting rid of Jameson yet. I was really coming to like him and the way he slept with his paw on my cheek. I'd be lonely without him in my apartment.

Sitting in a holding cell is boring. I was the only one in either cell, so I had no one to talk to. Occasionally, people came to check on me, but none of them were up for a chat. They didn't even tell me what time it was when I asked. Palmer, of course, had taken my phone and watch from me.

I'd used my one call to call Abby. There was no way I wanted my family to know I'd been arrested, not until after I'd already gotten myself out on bail. With luck, I'd never have to mention it at all. She said she'd call her parents for help finding me a lawyer and bail money.

What I thought was lunchtime came and went, but no one brought me anything.

I paced back and forth—a hundred diagonal lengths of the cell just for something to do. How did people in jail survive the boredom? First of all, they were fed regularly, and secondly, they saw more people than I had. I felt like I was more in solitary confinement.

The chief came in with a set of keys and unlocked my door.

"Lunch time?" I asked.

"No. It's time for you to go."

"Palmer arrested me. Don't I have to go to jail? Or try to post bail?"

He looked at me. "Are you saying you'd rather stay?"

"Oh no! Absolutely not. I guess I don't understand how all this works."

He looked around. "We can talk in my office."

Once he closed his office door, I sat. The office hadn't changed in the few months since I'd last been here. His brag wall was the same—no new photos or accolades. It must have been a slow season for him.

He had my belongings in a bag on his desk. "You can take your things back."

I put my watch on and saw it was only one in the afternoon. If I hadn't seen the sun through the windows on my way to the office, I would have sworn it was eight at night. "Thanks. How did you . . . ?"

"I didn't think Palmer was going to take my warning about leaving your family alone to heart. There's only so much I can do. He follows the evidence and does as he sees fit. I have to watch and clean up after him."

"How do you know I didn't kill Agatha?" I asked.

He smiled. "Look at you. You've got innocence written all over you. Plus, you had an alibi."

"Palmer said Abby wasn't good enough."

"Palmer didn't want Abby to be good enough. I called her, and she sounded credible to me."

"Thank you, I appreciate you standing up for me like this."

"I won't be able to for much longer though. Palmer has good instincts, and he knows there's something different about your family. He's going to keep digging until he figures something out. He's not looking in the right direction, so heaven only knows what he's going to come up with."

"Can't you clue him in a little more?" I asked.

His eyes went wide. "Absolutely not. Your aunts would do terrible things to me if I even considered it. Your family has to make the decision to take Palmer into their trust. For what it's worth, I think you should. Maybe you could suggest they ease him into it. He's a man of integrity, and he'd hold your secret to the grave."

I nodded. "I get that same feeling. I'll talk to the aunts."

"And speaking of your aunts, maybe we don't have to tell them about today?"

I laughed. "I was going to ask you the same thing. If they never hear I've been arrested, it would be best."

"Agreed. And, technically speaking, you haven't been arrested. I managed to catch Palmer before he finished the paperwork, so you were never in the system."

I let out a long sigh of relief. "Can I go now? I was supposed to meet with someone this morning, and I need to open the apothecary."

He stood up. "Of course. And if there's a next time, might I suggest you make me your first call?

Oh man! I can't believe I didn't think of that. "Definitely. Thank you."

I walked out as fast as I could, before he tried to get Palmer to drive me home or something. I needed to get to the apothecary and salvage as much as I could from my day.

Once I opened the apothecary, Abby stopped by with coffee and food.

"You're the best!" I said as I opened the bag from the Fancy Tart. Abby had brought enough food for at least two people: two egg sandwiches, two eclairs, a blueberry muffin, and a bear claw.

"Do you want some?" I asked.

She shook her head. "I'm sorry I couldn't help you. My parents went through the roof when I told them what you needed."

"I can imagine. But don't worry."

"Are you okay? I got weird calls from the police, and then you weren't there to meet Mrs. Thompson's son; I was worried."

"I'm fine. Thanks for being my alibi. If the chief hadn't called you, I'd probably still be in a holding cell."

"Wait, what? Did Palmer arrest you?"

I nodded. "Yes, but technically no. The chief stopped the paperwork before it went through, so there's no record of it."

"Your family must be really mad!"

I grinned. "Nope. They'll never know. They think Palmer was just asking me questions."

Abby frowned. "Please, promise me you'll stay out of trouble from now on."

"Technically, I wasn't in trouble, except on paper, and that's been destroyed now. It's like I never spent a few hours in a holding cell."

Abby frowned. "Are you sure about that?"

"Unless the chief lied to me, which I doubt, I have no police record." I wanted to change the subject. "Did you talk to Mrs. T.'s son?"

"I did. He didn't realize I knew who he was. He asked if I had Joshua, the cat. I told him no."

I was relieved she didn't give Jameson away. "Why didn't you give him the cat?" I asked.

"That's the weirdest thing. When he knocked on the door, Jameson hissed and ran off. I didn't really want to give our cat to some guy who couldn't even get his name right, so I said we didn't have one. He was upset, and then he asked me to step inside his mother's apartment and pick up a few things for him. I thought it was okay, since the crime scene tape was gone and Officer Papatonis wasn't standing there."

"Why didn't he go in himself?"

"I told him it would be much easier, but he said the apartment made him too sad, and it would be helpful if I went instead."

"What did he want?" I asked.

"He asked for her jewelry, for mementos, and her silver brush, comb and mirror set."

I nodded. "Did you notice how little she had? He asked for the only valuable things in the apartment. He strikes me as the kind of guy who would hawk it all for a little cash."

"I don't think so, he was really broken up that I couldn't find Jameson. He seemed more sentimental than that."

"Did he leave a number? I can call and arrange another pickup time."

"He said he'd try and stop by tonight, before he left town."

Once I got home, I stopped off at my landlord's to ask about my window.

Mrs. Subramanian answered the door. "Oh, Isabella, how are you? Not too shaken up still about that broken window, are you?"

"No, not much. I was wondering when it was going to be fixed, though."

"Manit is thinking about putting wrought iron across the window so you won't have to worry about a break-in ever again."

I could see my rent going up to pay for the extra security measures, which would make the apartment too expensive for Abby and me. "That's very thoughtful of him. This is my first apartment, and I don't know how this works. Is this something I would pay for? I only ask because I'm not sure I can afford much more than a pane of glass, or any kind of increase in my rent."

She opened her door wider. "Please, come in. I shouldn't have you standing out here in the hallway."

I walked into the apartment. I expected theirs to look much like mine, because all the apartments in the building had the same layout, but theirs was like a showroom. "Oh, how lovely!" I exclaimed. The deep teal walls practically glowed in the afternoon sunlight. Yellow accents and white furniture kept the room from being too dark.

"Thank you. Would you believe almost everything here was bought secondhand and restored? Manit is very good at that sort of thing."

I looked more closely at their furniture.

"Amazing."

She gestured to a white couch. "Please, sit down."

I wasn't sure that was a good idea. I wasn't the tidiest person, and a white couch sounded like a bad idea. What if I had a carrier oil on my pants and it soaked into the fabric?

"Please, don't worry. Let me get you something to drink."

Reluctantly, I sat on the corner of the couch.

She returned from the kitchen. "Cardamom iced coffee. Very delicately flavored—you'll love it."

Great. A brown drink to tempt my clumsiness. "Thank you."

She sat on a silk embroidered chair. "Your rent helps pay for incidentals like fixing the windows or upgrading the building's security. You aren't to be blamed if someone tries to break into your apartment. You and Abby are nice young women, quiet, don't cause trouble. After that horrible incident a few months ago, I told Manit to make sure you two were safer, but he didn't think anything like this would ever happen again. Let me tell you, as soon as he was done boarding up your window, I let him know under no circumstances would we allow the young women in our building to be threatened again."

I looked for a place to set my drink down, but the coffee table was too far away. "That's kind of you."

"First, he'll make your windows safe, then he's going to install a whole-building alarm with separate subsystems for each apartment. Alarms will ring directly at the police station and our apartment."

"I'm overwhelmed. Thank you very much. My family will feel much better about your new precautions as well. It must be difficult, looking after five separate apartments. You never know what might be happening in any one of them."

"Very true. On the other hand, sometimes we don't want to know what our tenants are doing in the privacy of their own homes."

I blushed. "I can see that."

I shifted on my seat. "I feel bad, thinking about Mrs. Thompson. The police said she died in the early evening. I think if we had known she was in trouble, maybe we could have done something. I wasn't home then, and I wondered if you or Mr. S. were home and knew . . ."

"I was home, but I heard nothing. No yelling, no scuffles, nothing."

"How about Mr. S.? He said he was here, too."

"Four nights ago? No, he was out with his bowling team. He and some friends bowl in a league, and this year they're doing quite well. He says if they put in enough extra practice, they might win the city championship. He didn't get home until just before midnight."

I took another sip of my coffee. She was right. The cardamom flavor was delicate, but held its own against the boldness of the dark roast coffee. "Absolutely delicious. How do you make it?"

"It's easy. I put a cardamom pod in the coffee filter, on top of the grounds. It can be dull, drinking the same coffee all the time."

"I have one more quick question and then I won't keep you any longer. Have you seen Mrs. Thompson's son? He was planning to stop by and take her cat."

She shook her head. "No, I haven't. If he had a key to her apartment, he wouldn't have needed to stop here first."

I frowned. "I was hoping he might have left his phone number with you. I missed him earlier."

I handed her my empty glass. "Thank you for the coffee, and for taking such good care of Abby and me."

Chapter 20

The next morning, I had an early breakfast date with Thea and Delia at The Fancy Tart.

"I'm lost. I don't know who to believe anymore, or who else to consider as a suspect," I said through a mouthful of bear claw.

Delia put down her coffee and started counting on her fingers. "Let's see, we've got Rosemarie, who owed Mrs. Thompson money, Mr. Subramanian, who lied about where he was the evening she was killed, and Eunice, who tried to blame you for Agatha's murder."

"I don't even have a suspect list for poor Agatha yet. I feel like we need to solve one murder before we move on to another."

"What if the two are connected?" Thea asked. "Maybe Agatha knew something and decided to investigate it herself, rather than tell us."

I realized I hadn't told my cousins about Agatha's apartment. "Palmer showed me pictures from her apartment and read me a bit of her journal. She was obsessed with me—pictures of me, of all of us, all over her apartment. She also called all the times she came here for breakfast times she ate with me and wrote that we had long talks. I only ever talked to her to get her order or encourage her to see Trina or a doctor, but she made it sound like we were best friends."

"Weird," Thea said.

"Sad. She was so lonely she had to make up a best friend. The day you took her to Sewall was probably the best day she'd had for a long time," Delia said.

I hadn't considered that. I was completely oblivious to her needs other than for potions, but at least her last day was a good one, until she was murdered anyway. I shook my head—these thoughts weren't going to help.

"We need to start eliminating people so we can focus on the more likely candidates. If we consider means, motive, opportunity, and ability, I think Rosemarie had the least going for her to kill Mrs. Thompson," Thea said

"I agree. And I can't see Eunice having the strength to choke a much younger woman to death," Delia said.

I looked at my watch. "I can squeeze in another visit to Rosemarie before work, if you drive."

We packed up our food and headed across town.

Rosemarie opened the door. "Oh, girls. What a surprise to see you. Is everything okay?" she asked.

"Not really. Can we come in?"

She looked back at her house. "I'd rather—"

"Great," Thea said as she pushed the door open.

To my surprise, there was nothing in the entryway, or the living room. No furniture, carpets, lights. Nothing. "Were you robbed?" I asked.

She sniffled. "No. I had an estate sale, and almost everything sold. I've got about enough to pay the bills my husband left me and maybe find an inexpensive apartment. After that, I should be able to live carefully on my social security."

I had no idea. No wonder she'd put off paying Mrs. T. for so long. "I have two questions for you, and then we'll be out of your hair."

"Yes?"

"Where did your aconite flowers go?"

"My what?"

"The purple flowers along the edge of the stone path."

"Oh." She looked like we just took her last happy memory.

"I cut all the flowers down from the garden and sold them to friends and neighbors. To make money. Everyone got the same arrangement, so the aconite went to about a dozen different houses."

I frowned. Her friends and neighbors were probably not the type to make their own herbal poison and then feed it to random women. "Thank you. I'm sorry you're going through such a difficult time."

"I would have paid Beatrice back, if she were still alive."

"Of course you would have. But I think now she'd want you to keep the money."

Rosemarie smiled. "That's kind of you to say. And your second question?"

"Where were you the night Beatrice was killed, between five and seven?"

"I know I avoided this question the last time you asked. I was embarrassed and didn't want to tell you I was meeting with my bankruptcy advisor. I didn't tell the police about him. Do you think that matters?"

"I think it does. If you give Detective Palmer a call and tell him the truth, you'll be okay."

I saw Delia's lips tighten into a thin line at this. She might not like him very much, but he really was a good guy—even though he kept thinking I was a murderer.

Chapter 21

I waited across the street from my apartment, keeping an eye out for Mr. Subramanian to leave the building. I had no idea if he would be leaving tonight, so I was prepared to wait for a few hours if necessary.

I wasn't sure how far I'd be able to follow him on foot, but with the number of stop lights and signs in our neighborhood, I thought I could keep up for a while. If I needed to, I could tail him again two nights from now.

After waiting for fifteen minutes and seriously rethinking my life choices, Mr. Subramanian left the building and climbed into his car. He turned left out of the parking lot and, thankfully, didn't seem to be in much of a hurry. I started to jog after him. Would he think it was suspicious that I was jogging tonight when I hadn't even put my sneakers on in a couple months?

Lisa Bouchard

Hopefully he wasn't paying enough attention to my exercise program to notice.

I kept him in sight for four blocks, then he turned right onto Thaxter Road. I sped up despite the complaint from my lungs. Four blocks isn't much of a jog, and they should be quiet and do their job.

They didn't listen and kept complaining.

I turned on Thaxter and saw Mr. Subramanian's car parked halfway down the street. Instantly, my legs decided they didn't need this kind of abuse anymore and slowed to a walk.

My lungs applauded this decision.

I needed to get more exercise—I couldn't let a short half-mile jog exhaust me.

I got to the house and decided an invisibility spell wasn't necessary. It was a dark, moonless night, and the fewer spells I cast, the fewer ways I'd have to screw them up.

I could see Mr. S. in the window of the house he parked in front of. A blonde woman in her thirties handed him a drink. He took it and smiled warmly at her.

He handed her an envelope, and she hugged him.

What was going on here? Mr. S. was in his early sixties, and she could be his daughter. Was she his daughter? The blonde hair seemed to say no.

She wasn't letting him go, though. Maybe she was having an affair with him? That seemed unlikely, but if there was money in the envelope...people will do a lot for money.

A tall man walked into the living room and smiled at the hugging couple.

I stood a little straighter so I could see more of the room.

Behind the tall man was a young boy with his mother's hair and his father's dark skin. The boy rushed to Mr. S., who let go of the woman and threw the boy gently up into the air.

This was a family scene. Looking closer at the younger man, I realized he could easily be Mr. Subramanian's son. So he was here visiting his son's family.

Why wouldn't he tell his wife? This would have to be a question for another day.

I stretched to relieve the growing kink in my back and caught the eye of the German shepherd that had been laying on the couch.

His ears lifted and he barked, staring right at me.

I couldn't hear anyone in the house, but I imagined they took the warnings of their guard dog seriously. I threw up a hasty invisibility spell, hoping I could get out of the yard and far enough down the street before the dog convinced his owners to let him out.

The front door to the house opened, and I heard the man say, "It's probably just a cat." The dog ran out and bounded toward me.

I thought he was going to leap at me. I crossed my arms in front of my face for protection and braced for the impact. When he was two feet from me, he stopped, cocked his head and looked confused. I held my breath and considered my options. I could stay where I was and hope the dog moved along, or I could slowly move away and hope he didn't hear me. Either way, I didn't like relying on hope to keep me safe.

I took one experimental step toward the sidewalk. The dog matched my step, but didn't come any closer or look any less confused.

I took another, very large step. So did the dog.

The sidewalk was three more steps away, and two more steps away there was a row of neatly planted flags.

I took the last three steps out of the yard with a pounding heart, because the dog was looking less confused and more inclined to bite me.

He stopped at two steps.

"Lacy, come back in," his owner cried.

Lacy, who was a beautiful dog now that she wasn't trying to sniff me out, turned to the house.

"Come on, girl. It was just a squirrel."

She gave one last look at the space I was standing in, and then trotted to the door.

I let out a long, quiet sigh of relief and started to walk home. Once I turned the corner, I allowed my invisibility spell to evaporate while I was standing in the unlit spot between two street lights.

I could cross Mr. S. off my list of suspects. He had a secret, but not one he'd kill for, and not one I'd be willing to tell his wife about.

Chapter 22

I I didn't want to go into work, but I didn't really have a choice. I made a mental note to ask my accountant to let me know the minute I could afford to hire an assistant.

I finished making potions for Jameson, Mrs. Newcomb, and a new client, Amber Drysdale. Amber was one of my youngest clients, probably in her mid-twenties. There wasn't much wrong with her, other than the stress of working full-time, raising a six-year-old daughter, and wondering whether her husband was cheating on her or not. I imagine that could give anyone headaches.

I placed this new stock on the shelf beneath the cash register and was about to go into my office for lunch when the door chimes rang. I looked up and saw Kate, looking uncertain, standing in the doorway.

"Kate, come on in."

She was in civilian clothes, and this was the first time I had seen her out of uniform. Her long brown hair was down and fell below her shoulders. She was wearing jeans and a green tank top that showed off her muscular arms. She frowned and hesitated for a moment before she seemed to make up her mind and muster her will. She strode up to the back counter. "We need to talk."

I bit my tongue and tried to smile. "I know. I'm really sorry—"

"I think it's best if you let me talk first," Kate said.

I nodded. She was right, I had upset her. She should get everything off her chest before I started to apologize. "Do you want to go sit in my office?"

"First, I wanted to say I'm sorry about your friend, Agatha. Finding two dead friends in a week must be difficult."

Two dead friends in a week. Three dead friends in a few months. It didn't seem very safe to be my friend these days.

"Thank you. I appreciate that."

Kate followed me into my office and sat down. "I need to know you understand what you did was wrong and promise it will never happen again."

I nodded.

"I've been thinking about this for a while, and you hurt my feelings because you didn't trust me enough to tell me what you were doing." She ran her hands through her long hair. "I mean, what did you think I'd do, if you said you were going to go and look for Abby yourself?"

I sighed. Here's where I had to be careful with my explanation. I wasn't even close to being ready to explain my family's past, or our talents, to her. "I thought if I told you we were going out to find Abby, you'd call Palmer and try to keep me safe in the apartment. I couldn't do that—I couldn't just sit there and hope Palmer would find her. He had no idea where to look, and if I left it to him, who knows when he might have found her."

"Yes, well, that's my job. It's my job to protect the public and find the bad guys. You took both those things away from me. You remember why I joined the police, how finding criminals gives my life meaning. In giving me the sleeping tea, you took the meaning of my life away from me."

Ooof. That hurt. "I didn't think about it like that on the night, but I can see why you think that way. I am really sorry. I didn't mean for this to have any repercussions, I was desperate and afraid and felt like I couldn't control anything. I needed to go out and look for her and nothing else but my best friend mattered to me at that moment."

I let her think about what I said for a moment and continued. "You know that feeling, where you desperately have to go out and do something, anything, to help."

Kate nodded. "I do."

"And I promise I will be completely honest and up front with you from now on."

Now it was Kate's turn to sigh. "I don't know whether to believe you or not."

"That's understandable. Maybe we could call this a second chance, and you could put me on probation?"

Kate smiled. "You're definitely on probation. I'd tell you not to investigate what happened to Agatha, but I doubt you'd listen to me."

I smiled.

"The thing is, if you have police with you, you're going to be safer. My badge and gun can keep you safer than you'd be on your own."

I definitely wasn't going to tell her that wasn't true.

"So I hope you'll call me when you find things that need to be investigated. I can understand why you might not want to call Palmer, so just call me."

"I promise to think about it," I said. Before she could reply, I continued. "You look like your head still hurts. Can I help?"

"Yes. Please. The feverfew helps, but the headaches aren't completely going away."

I looked at her, and my senses showed me what she really needed for healing was more rest and less stress. "So here's the thing. You need to change up your lifestyle a bit. You're never going to get rid of them if you continue to get too little sleep and allow too much stress to build up."

"You can tell that?"

"It just takes one look at you to see you're not sleeping enough, and what sleep you're getting isn't restful. I can give you more feverfew, but you need to start deliberately relaxing. You can meditate, or do yoga, or even beat out your stress on a punching bag, whatever allows you to let go and relax."

"The punching bag sounds good. I'll sleep better, too, if I pound on it for a while."

I smiled. "Good. I've got some feverfew in the shop."

She followed me to the wall of ready-made tinctures. I took one bottle of feverfew and infused it with my will for her headaches to go away.

"This is on the house, as long as you tell me what you're going to do for stress relief today."

She thought for a moment. "I'm going to the gym. I'll run for a couple miles then hit the punching bag."

"That sounds like a good start. And because I'm such a pain, I won't take it personally if you imagine you're taking your frustrations out on me."

"You're not so much a pain, as an overly enthusiastic citizen, and I'd never hit you. The idea is just wrong."

I laughed. "That's good to know."

She turned toward the door. "Don't forget, call me before you investigate."

I didn't say I would, but I didn't say I wouldn't either.

Chapter 23

After work, I spent some time at the Dollar Store picking up supplies. I felt like I couldn't figure out who did what and when without some kind of diagram.

I hesitated calling it a murder board, because that sounded way too gruesome, but that's what it was. I hoped I could also work out if the two recent murders in my life were somehow related.

On the way home, my mother called. I considered not answering, because I couldn't take any more bad news. I picked up anyway.

"Hi, Mom. What's up?"

"Hi sweetie. I've been meaning to ask you, but this last week has been so tragic, I haven't found a good time. How was your date?"

I sighed. "Oh my goddess, Mom. You didn't warn me he was, well, I guess unmotivated is the nicest thing I can say."

"What do you mean?"

I stopped walking for a moment. "All he wants to do is spend time with his friends and drink beer. He can't go out on weekends because all he does is watch sports at his friends' houses and drink beer."

"That doesn't sound so bad," my mother said.

"Oh no, I haven't told you the best part yet. He's at his friends' all weekend because he's too drunk to drive anywhere."

My mother didn't respond.

"You still there?"

"Yes. I didn't realize he, uh…Well, anyway, you certainly don't have to see him again."

"Maybe you can let me find my own dates from now on?"

"You're not getting any younger, you know. It takes a while to find the right man, settle down and be ready to have children. You've got a little less than seven years."

This was an argument I never won with my mother, so I certainly wasn't going to get into it with her on the phone. "I can't talk about this right now. I'll try to keep an open mind, but dating isn't the most important thing I've got going on, not by a long shot."

I got home before Abby and started to set up boards in my room. I replaced the watercolors of the gardens at Prescott Park from one wall with the foam board I'd bought.

I printed out images of victims and suspects, and it didn't take long to cut them out and write the pertinent facts below them. I used different colored highlighters to link similar ideas together, and by the time I was done, I thought I had everything organized.

Abby came home and peeked into my room. "What's that?"

"I'm having a hard time visualizing everything that's going on in the case, and I'm trying to get a handle on it."

She looked from the board, to me, then back to the board. "You promised me you'd stay out of trouble."

I had promised. And I had stayed out of trouble since then. "I haven't gotten into any trouble, though. I'm just trying to figure this all out."

"And while you've been trying to figure things out, our apartment has been broken into, and another woman you know was killed. When is it going to end, Isabella?"

I stood up and gave her a hug. I hated when she got so upset. Correction. When I made her so upset. Still, I felt I owed her the truth. "I don't know. I don't know how long it will take me to figure out who killed Mrs. Thompson, or Agatha."

She struggled out of my grasp and wiped her eyes. "I can't take it anymore. I was barely starting to feel safe here, then"—she gestured wildly—"all this started to happen again."

"I'm sorry. Tell me what you want me to do."

She rubbed the last of the tears away. "I want you to stop. Let the police handle it and go back to living a quiet life. You're so obsessed with solving these crimes that we don't even do anything together anymore. I want you to be my best friend, not some crime solver who brings danger to our apartment."

I frowned. "I don't think I can do that." I wanted to tell her why, tell her that I was doing my best to protect Kate and Palmer and her from the witches who had started to use magic for evil and selfish reasons. I wished I could, but I knew she wouldn't accept what I had to say.

Sometimes it hurt, knowing I couldn't be myself with my best friend, but there were no other witches in school with me except Thea and Delia, so there was no one I could have picked for a best friend who would have dealt well with the truth. I had to do the best I could with the friend I had.

"If you can't stop, then I have to leave. I can't stay here, terrified every night that someone will break in or try to kill us."

My heart sank. "You didn't tell me you were so afraid."

"And you never asked. How do you think I felt after being kidnapped? Did it even occur to you that the break-in would bring up all my fears again?"

I tried to pull her into a hug, but she stepped back from me. "I knew you were afraid, but you never said anything. I didn't want to bring it up if you didn't want to talk about it, so I let you decide when you wanted to talk. I guess I shouldn't have done that."

177

"It doesn't matter now. I'm going to pack some clothes and go to my parents' house."

I didn't want her to go, but I had to let her. "You'll be safe there. And I hope you're able to relax there too."

She turned and walked out of my room. I stayed where I was, until I heard the apartment door slam.

An hour later, Thea and Delia came in with Indian takeout for dinner.

"Does Abby want some?" Thea asked.

"She's moved out," I said morosely.

"What? No way!"

"Yeah, she saw my murder board and freaked out."

"Poor kid. I don't think she's made for this sort of thing," Delia said.

We dished out the food and sat at the table.

"Since she's not here, I guess there's no reason not to hang the board on the wall out here," I said.

After I hung it up on the dining area wall, we surveyed it while we ate.

"I'm not seeing any real connection between Agatha and Mrs. Thompson," Thea said.

"Me neither," I agreed.

"You know who I think is missing up here?" Delia asked.

I shook my head.

"Her son. Think about it. It makes perfect sense to me. The amulet is usually handed down in families, but he found out he's not getting it. He's really mad and decides to take it for himself, only she won't give it to him. Desperate, he kills her, thinking he can find it in the apartment once she's gone. Only he can't," Delia said.

"Sounds plausible," I said.

"How does Agatha come into play here?" Thea asked.

"Agatha saw him in Sewall. Maybe she saw something we didn't? What if she confronted him when he came back to town? He'd have to kill her to keep his secret."

I pulled out another sheet of paper and tacked it onto the board. I wrote out Delia's ideas and then sat back, staring at everything up on the wall.

"It makes sense. But poison? It's usually a woman's murder method."

"And strangling is a man's. I don't think the poison rules him out, not nearly as much as strangling would rule out Eunice," Thea said.

"I suppose so."

A loud knock at my door startled me. I looked out the peephole and saw Grandma. I unlocked the door and let her in. To my surprise, Eunice walked in behind her.

Chapter 24

I furrowed my brow as they made themselves comfortable in the living room, moving dining chairs around and even grabbing the chair from my bedroom. All women. Why did it seem like there were hardly ever any men in my life? "You!" I said, staring at Eunice. "You told the police I was at your house with the body. Why would you do that to me?"

She sat on my couch and said, "The detective threatened to put me in jail. I can't be locked up, not when I've got to make sure Beatrice's killer is found."

"But it's okay for me to be in jail?" I shot back.

"I knew he'd never keep you there, and I was right," Eunice said.

"It's time to put an end to this nonsense," Grandma said, waving her hand toward my murder board on the dining room wall. I had put everyone on it, even if I'd already determined they weren't Mrs.

Thompson's killer, because I had no idea who had killed Agatha.

Eunice laughed. "I don't know whether to be insulted or flattered that you think I've got it in me to kill someone at this age."

I blushed. "I don't really think you killed Agatha, but I had to consider all options."

Eunice nodded. "Sensible girl you've got there, Esther."

Grandma cleared her throat as she inspected the board. "You're down to two suspects, Mr. Subramanian and Brent."

"I'm really just down to Brent, but I can't imagine he'd kill his own mother. Mr. Subramanian is keeping a secret from his wife, but he's no killer. I need to come up with some more suspects."

"Of course it's the son," Grandma said. "Rent isn't enough motive, your landlord could have just had her thrown out."

"I haven't ruled out Eunice for Mrs. Thompson's murder, though."

Grandma laughed. "Eunice, tell her."

Eunice stood up and started pacing my small living room. "You know about the Bishop amulet, right?"

I nodded. "I haven't been able to find it yet."

"Well, I have the Lynch amulet."

"Lynch?" I asked.

"Each amulet is named for the original family that held it."

Oh! Somehow I had thought, because Mrs. T. had the Bishop amulet, that they all had a religious designation.

"Why didn't you tell us that when we were at your house?" Thea asked.

"Witches who hold the amulets try to keep it a secret," Eunice said.

"No witch can hold more than one amulet, it's too much of a drain."

"So that's why she's not a suspect," said Grandma.

I was feeling contrary. "That may explain why she wouldn't have killed Mrs. T., but it doesn't say anything about whether she murdered Agatha."

Eunice's face turned red. "Holders of amulets protect witches; they don't kill them."

"So someone else has the Bishop amulet?" I asked.

"According to Hope, it hasn't been found yet," Grandma said.

"Things aren't any better in Sewall yet?" Thea asked.

Grandma shook her head. "Hope says the roads are almost impassable by car, and half the trees in town are fully dead."

I was at a loss for what to do. "I guess we could search Mrs. Thompson's apartment again. I doubt we'll come up with any new clues, though."

"We don't need to search. The amulets are attuned to each other, and mine can find yours," Eunice said.

"Are we really sure it should be mine?" I asked.

"Once we find it, we'll see."

She pulled her amulet out from under her shirt. It was a deep red garnet in a silver setting. She took it off her neck. "It will glow when we point it in the right direction."

She stood up and slowly turned in a circle. The amulet glowed when pointed toward the back of the apartment. She led the way, and we followed her to the bathroom.

"It's in here, somewhere."

Grandma opened the medicine cabinet, and I opened the towel closet. Neither of us found it.

"Check everything on the shelves," Eunice commanded. The small bookshelf next to the sink only held a couple cleaning supplies and no amulet.

I looked at the litter box. "You don't think . . ."

"Try the clean litter first. Just in case," Grandma said.

I took a trash bag from the shelf and poured the clean litter into it. No sense wasting it. No amulet fell out, but when I shook the box, I heard a chain rattling. I ripped the top off the box, and there it was, taped to the side of the box.

I yanked the gold chain and held it up, the emerald stone shining in its gold setting for Grandma and Eunice to see. "This is it, right?"

They nodded.

"Give it a quick rinse," Eunice commanded.

"What does the water do?" I asked.

Eunice smirked. "It washes away the kitty litter. Not everything in life has a mystical quality to it."

I grinned at her, but felt a little silly.

After I rinsed the amulet, I wrapped it in a hand towel to dry.

"Maybe we can talk more outside the bathroom," Grandma said.

I followed them back to the living room. "You girls are going to have to leave now," Eunice said.

Thea and Delia both looked like they wanted to protest, but—at a glare from Grandma—gave me a quick hug instead. "Tell us everything later, okay?" Thea said.

I nodded and they left quickly, before I even had time to say anything.

"Got any coffee?" Eunice asked.

"Yes. I apologize for not offering you some right away. I've got cookies, too, if you want some."

"I'd love some," Grandma said.

I slipped a cardamom pod into my coffee filter along with the grounds and put a half dozen oatmeal raisin cookies on a small plate. These cookies were the last thing Abby made here. Once this case was over, I was going to have to apologize to her.

"You're about to join the Sorority of Brigid."

"Brigid?"

Eunice looked at Grandma. "What did you teach this girl?"

Grandma looked sheepish. "Her mother wanted to give her more grounding in the non-magic world."

Eunice frowned. "You should have stepped in and put a stop to that."

184

Grandma frowned back at Eunice. "If I'd thought any of my girls would have to deal with this burden, then I would have."

Eunice turned to me. "Brigid is the goddess of poetry, fertility, and protection. Those of us who carry amulets call on her to protect us."

"There are hundreds across the country, thousands across the world, but for now we should just focus on the local ones here in New Hampshire. There are seven of us, and usually we don't know who the others are. It's better that way since, as you have seen, people try to steal them occasionally. If anyone knew where a large number of them were, it would be easy to take that power."

I took a cookie. "I see."

"We're directly in opposition to the Fraternity of Free Witches."

I furrowed my brow. "Never heard of them."

Eunice stole a glance at Grandma. "I'm not surprised. Living down here, you don't hear as much about the bad things happening in the supernatural world."

"I guess not." In fact, I hadn't heard much about the supernatural world at all, outside of what directly impacted me. I wondered if the aunts had kept it that way on purpose.

"What have I been missing?"

"The fraternity is growing and getting bolder, while the sorority has a fixed number. If the fraternity manages to take the amulets, they'll be able to do some unspeakable things."

"But I thought you said the amulet wouldn't let me wear it if I wasn't the right one. How could someone else take or use one?"

"With enough persuasion, a witch could be forced to choose someone else to hand it down to."

I shuddered. Magic in the wrong hands was bad. Organized magic bent on doing wrong could ruin the world.

"So what do I have to do?"

At this moment, Eunice's phone rang. The witch's cackle ringtone startled me, and I jumped.

"I know, it's a little on the nose, but it makes me smile," Eunice said by way of apology.

"Hope? Is everything alright?"

She paused for a moment to listen. "Okay. I was hoping for another day or so to get the girl used to the idea, but we can do it now. Give me a couple minutes."

She hung up and turned to me. "I wanted to wait, give you some time, but buildings are collapsing in Sewall. Put the amulet on."

I picked it up from the coffee table, looked at it and raised it over my head. The chain slid over my head easily, and the amulet felt cool on my skin.

Eunice breathed out a heavy sigh. "Good. Things should start getting better now."

I turned toward her and felt my amulet glow. I know that sounds weird, but it was like I could feel the light on my skin.

From behind me, I heard a man's voice. "It's about time you figured it out."

Chapter 25

Eunice peered behind me. "This must be your familiar."

Jameson jumped up on my lap and sat. Was it my imagination, or did he seem even more haughty than usual? "Jameson, at your service."

Eunice slowly nodded to him with a sense of reverence I did not understand. "Do you also accept her?"

"I do," he said.

Grandma nodded. She stood up and kissed me on the forehead. "You've made me proud, Isabella. We'll leave the two of you to get acquainted."

I rubbed my face with my hands. How had my life gotten so weird all of a sudden?

Once Eunice and Grandma, who had been surprisingly quiet, left, Jameson said, "Listen up, buttercup. There's a lot to do and not a lot of time to do it in. Right now I'm the one with the most experience here, and you should listen to me."

"But you're a cat," I said.

"I'm a talking cat who knows who murdered Beatrice, and who will train you to use the amulet effectively. I'm over two hundred years old, and you're lucky I'm not making you call me sir."

I blinked. "Two hundred?"

He licked his paw and cleaned his face. "Over two hundred. Meaning ten times your age, ten times your experience, and at least ten times your wisdom."

Ten times my snarkiness, too, it seemed. "Okay then, great wise familiar, enlighten me."

"That's substantially better. You are right, it was Brent who killed Beatrice. He won't give up trying to get the amulet, so we need to find him first and get him out of the way."

That sounded ominous. "What do you mean, get him out of the way? I can't kill people, you know."

"Don't be silly. Of course you can. You may not want to—and with any luck, you may not need to—but some people have dedicated their lives to so much evil that there's nothing left to do but kill them before they intentionally harm even more people."

"No jail time? No rehabilitation? No mind wipes to reset them on the right course?"

Cats can't laugh, but I swore he laughed at me anyway. "The people we're talking about, like Brent, are far beyond that point. Evil is in their nature, and there's no way to scrub it out."

"I don't believe you."

"You will, someday. Brigid protect that you don't find out too late."

"Explain how the amulet works. Do I need to go to Sewall to make sure the damage isn't continuing?"

"No. The fact you're wearing it is enough."

I stood up and paced the room. "I don't feel any different. I can't feel things or see anything differently."

Okay, it's official. Cats can laugh. Jameson wasn't doing me any favors in the self-esteem department here. "Give it time. You're talking to me now. I've been trying to talk to you for days, hoping the amulet was close enough to you, but it wasn't working."

I looked at him and pursed my lips. "Were you calling my name? I thought I heard someone, maybe outside, yelling for me, but I couldn't ever find anyone."

"Yes, that was me. It would have taken months for me to break through to you without the amulet."

"And now you're my familiar? Are you sure there hasn't been some kind of mistake? I mean, aren't you supposed to be a really powerful witch to get a familiar?"

"In order of your questions, yes, yes, and yes."

"So what do I do now? If I'm supposed to be some great witch, I shouldn't just continue to be me, should I?"

"I don't understand your question," he said.

"I'm just normal. Sort of ordinary, kind of clumsy, not very remarkable. I don't understand why Mrs. T. picked me."

Who knew cats could sigh in exasperation?

"You have everything you need to fulfill your destiny. Perhaps you shouldn't worry so much. It's my job to guide you, and I haven't ever lost a young witch."

"Stress less? I've got a murderer to find, a roommate to apologize to, a business to run, and now apparently I've got a destiny to fulfill." I sat down on the couch. "It's too much to deal with."

I really wanted to eat eclairs, watch Star Wars movies, and ignore destiny. Unfortunately, my phone rang. Caller ID said Brent Thompson. Why was he calling me? Did he want to get caught?

"Are you going to answer that, maybe catch him?" Jameson asked.

I answered the phone. "I know you killed your mother."

"It took you long enough to figure it out. But if I were you, I wouldn't worry so much about what I did to my mother, as much as what I'll do to yours if you don't bring me the amulet."

I looked to Jameson, but he was scratching behind his ear.

"If you touch my mother—"

"Don't worry. I don't even have her yet. If you bring me the amulet, I never will."

"I don't believe you."

"That's wise. But with the amulet, I'll have far too much to do to worry about your family, and if you're lucky, I'll never even think of the Proctors again."

"Who says I even have the amulet?"

"I've got friends in Sewall. They know someone has it, because the trees have stopped dying. You've got the cat, so that means my mother has chosen you. Put it all together, and that amulet is around your neck right now."

"Even if I had it, I wouldn't give it to you."

"That's certainly a choice you can make. Let me just pull up directions to Proctor House. I'm sure your mother is there this late in the evening. Maybe she's helping your Aunt Nadia in the kitchen. But perhaps I'll run into your grandmother first. She's old, I doubt she'd be able to fight me off for long."

"Don't you dare!" I said.

"I won't have to, as long as I have what I need."

"And do you want Jameson, too?"

He scoffed. "No. I'll find my own familiar. Maybe a nice scorpion. I think that would suit my personality much more."

"Fine. But we meet in public, in the daytime. I don't trust you."

"Probably best you don't. Prescott Park, noon tomorrow. Leave the amulet hanging on the trident on the water fountain."

"You're not worried someone will see it?"

"Of course not. You're smart enough to make it invisible."

"Noon. It will be there."

"And Isabella, don't let me see you there, or our deal is off."

Chapter 26

It goes without saying that the first thing I did was go to Proctor House with Jameson. My family was stunned that I volunteered to stay the night after I explained what Brent wanted.

They welcomed Jameson to the house, and even made plans to have a cat door put in for him. I was amazed at the fuss they made over him, just because he was over two hundred years old and knew more than the rest of us. He loved all the attention, too.

Between the eight of us, we managed to come up with what we hoped was a foolproof plan and went to bed, because we all had to be at the park before the sun came up in the morning.

My alarm went off at four, and I groaned.

"Not a morning person, I see," Jameson said.

I screamed, because I thought there was a strange man in my bedroom.

Thea rushed into my room, carrying a baseball bat. "What is it?" she asked.

"Sorry. It's just Jameson. I'm not used to him, and I thought someone was in my room."

"Someone was in your room. Me," he said.

"Someone human, a stranger," I explained.

We ate a quick, silent breakfast and headed out to the park. Grandma checked for traps but found none. Good, we were there before he was.

I hung the amulet on the trident, and then Delia made it, and me, invisible. The aunts and my cousins would take turns walking through the park with different glamours, mimicking tourists. Grandma held a spell that kept non-magic people away from the park. She'd be exhausted holding it until noon, so Aunt Nadia would take over if necessary.

Jameson took up his position in a tree, watching for Brent.

Now all we had to do was settle in and wait.

At eleven thirty, I started to get very antsy. "Stop moving around so much, Isabella," Delia chided as she walked by. "It's not easy to keep you invisible when you're moving."

I moved back to my spot under a tree—easier for Delia, because she didn't have to hide my shadow as well—and stood still.

"He's entering the park," Jameson said. To anyone but my family, he would just sound like a cat yowling.

Brent took a slow, leisurely walk through the park, enjoying the flowers and admiring the view across the river. At noon, he approached the fountain. With one flick of his wrist, he dissolved the invisibility spell and picked up the amulet.

He turned and saw me. Delia had used the same spell to keep the amulet and me invisible. Instantly, I was blinded by light.

His spell wore off as Grandma and the aunts ran toward us. "What happened?"

"He saw us."

"Where is he?" I asked.

Grandma pointed to an exit. "That way."

Jameson and I ran to the cousins' car and scrambled into it. They relied on a ward to keep people from stealing the car and even went so far as to keep the electronic key in the glove box.

"He's in a black Escalade," Jameson said. We looked around and saw him peeling out of a parking spot and driving down Marcy Street. Our car was smaller and took the narrow roads of old Portsmouth better than his, but he didn't seem to care about sideswiping any cars in his way. We followed him in a low-speed chase through Market Square to Middle Street, where he started to gain distance.

From out of nowhere, a police cruiser pulled in between us and Brent, and another appeared behind us, both with lights and sirens on.

"I've got to pull over."

"No! We've got to catch him," Jameson said.

The cruiser in front of us forced Brent to the side of the road, and I waited as long as I could before pulling over.

Kate approached Brent's car. "No, Kate! Stop!" I yelled, but our windows were up, and she didn't hear me.

Brent rolled down his window. Kate stopped behind the car and called in his license plate.

I tried to open my door, but it was blocked by Officer Papatonis. "Let me out! Kate's in danger!" I yelled at him.

He stepped away from my door, and I pushed it open. "Miss Proctor?"

"Kate," was all I could say as I watched her fall to the ground, too far away to help.

"Stay here, both of you," Palmer commanded. I hadn't seen him behind my car. He ran toward Kate and drew his weapon.

I threw up a very hasty protection spell for Kate and hoped Brent wouldn't hurt her again.

Brent backed up his car to get back into traffic, and as he did, Palmer shot the two back tires of the Escalade.

Brent continued to drive, but with the tires blown out, he wasn't getting very far. He sped off, faster than I thought he would be able to, but when he tried to take a corner, the back of the SUV fishtailed, and he hit a telephone pole.

Palmer bent down to check Kate.

I looked at Papatonis. "Can we go help?"

"You stay here. I'll go."

I stayed at the car and dropped the shield on Kate, but Jameson jumped out and ran toward the Escalade. He sat on the sidewalk directly across from Brent and swished his tail. On the third swish, the telephone pole split up the middle and fell across the street. Live wires sparked on the road, and all traffic came to a stop.

What kind of power did my familiar have, anyway?

Moments later, fire and emergency medical vehicles swarmed the area. Kate was taken away in an ambulance, still looking unresponsive.

An Eversource utility truck came and turned the power off. Brent was still dazed from the impact of the airbag. He tried to open the door to his car, but couldn't seem to manage it. Jameson sat completely still, staring at him until Palmer approached the Escalade.

I left my car and walked closer to the accident, prepared to shield Palmer from any spell Brent could cast. I could feel the Bishop amulet reaching out, trying to get back to me. Ordinarily, I wouldn't be a match for a witch more than twice my age, but the amulet lent me strength, even at this distance.

Palmer opened the Escalade's door and yanked Brent out of it. Brent fell out and stumbled on the ground. I felt him gathering his power, but he dropped it when Jameson hissed.

Palmer pulled him back up and pressed him against the car. "What did you do to Kate?"

Brent pulled his focus from Jameson to Palmer. "What do you mean? She fainted, didn't she?"

In one smooth motion, Palmer turned Brent around and had one handcuff on him. He grabbed Brent's other arm and tightened the other cuff on his wrist.

Palmer locked Brent in the back of Kate's cruiser and then walked to me. "What were you doing? You could have killed someone, driving so recklessly."

"He stole something from me. A necklace. Is it possible to get it back?" I asked.

Palmer shook his head. "You should know better. Jewelry isn't worth a life."

"But where is it?" I asked.

Palmer looked back at the Escalade. "Papatonis has got it in an evidence bag. What's this really about?"

"I can't tell you. Just be careful with it, please."

"You're going to have to come down to the station. Can I trust you to drive yourself? You'll be between the two cruisers and won't have an opportunity to break away."

I nodded.

He lowered his voice. "Isabella, don't try anything. I'll arrest you if you put one toe out of line."

"I understand. I'll see you there." There was no way I was going to leave Palmer alone with Brent if I could help it.

The amulet, still with Papatonis, let me feel Brent's attempts at magic. He was still too dazed from the air bag to focus his will, though.

I reached out and put my hand on Palmer's arm. "Please, watch out for him. He's dangerous."

"Of course he is," Palmer snapped at me.

That stung, but I didn't let go of his arm. "No, really. Promise you'll be on your guard."

He stared into my eyes. "This isn't like you. You run headlong into danger without even thinking about it."

"Then take my warning seriously."

He nodded and turned back to Kate's car.

Jameson jumped back into my car where my family was waiting for me.

"How did you get here so fast?" I asked Aunt Lily.

"Desperate times call for desperate measures. I hope your mother's Forget Me spell worked, and people don't start talking about the six women racing down the street."

Thea started the car, and we followed Palmer.

I turned to the back seat, crowded with the aunts. "Brent's still stunned from the airbag, but once we get to the station, we need to be on our guard. He'll try to steal the amulet and escape."

"I'm ready for him. There have been too many attacks on older witches in town, and I'm not letting him get away with this," Grandma said.

"Mother, you're getting paranoid," Aunt Lily said.

"I'm not sure she is," Aunt Nadia said. "First there was the tea she got in the spring, then Beatrice's murder. It could be the start of a pattern."

I thought about that for a moment. Was the fraternity trying to kill the older, stronger witches, or were these two isolated incidents?

Jameson meowed to get our attention. "If you'd like an expert opinion on the matter, you'll need another amulet for any hope of keeping him under control. Call Eunice."

Grandma pulled out her phone and, surprisingly, called Eunice. I had no idea they knew each other well enough for Grandma to have her number on speed dial. But then again, Grandma kept her knowledge of Eunice and her amulet to herself this whole time too.

"Eunice? It's Esther. We need two sorority members at the police station. I've got Isabella, but her amulet is in an evidence bag." She nodded. "Yes, right now."

She hung up and sighed. "That woman is too old to keep the amulet, but too stubborn to give it away."

"She doesn't have family to give it to?"

Grandma shook her head. "No. Her only daughter died decades ago. The rest of her family want nothing to do with it, or her."

Chapter 27

T hea pulled into the rear parking lot of the police station and parked two spots away from where Palmer parked Kate's cruiser.

Jameson and I met him at the back of the car.

"Isabella, you're with me. The rest of you need to wait out in the reception area."

My family started walking to the front door, and I turned to follow Palmer.

He adjusted his grip on Brent's arm, and the moment he let go, Brent disappeared. Batwings!

"No!" I yelled and my family turned around. "He's gone!"

Papatonis, who was walking toward us, fell backward.

"Fly to me," Brent said, and the evidence bag holding the Bishop amulet rose up out of Papatonis's hand before disappearing.

"What the?" Papatonis yelled.

Although he was invisible, I could hear Brent's footsteps as he ran past my family. We followed, Palmer shouting questions none of us wanted to answer.

My mother yelled "Stop him," which might have sounded like a normal command, but I could feel the spell she'd woven into the words.

She missed, because his footsteps kept pounding away from us. The tree to her left, however, stopped swaying in the breeze.

We saw a pair of broken handcuffs drop to the ground and adjusted course to follow Brent.

Aunt Lily, seeing what my mother did, yelled another disguised spell. "Show me!"

Brent flickered into visibility for a moment and stumbled, but quickly righted himself and kept running.

The empty evidence bag seemingly popped into existence and floated in the air.

My vision went dark, and I heard screaming in my head. The amulet was in pain, and I could feel Brent trying to force it over his head as he continued to run.

The amulet struggled, and Jameson surged ahead of us and leapt into the air. He landed on Brent, but looked like he was floating. Brent had stopped running, trying to shake Jameson off.

Jameson bit Brent, who howled and shook the cat free.

"Show me!" Grandma yelled. Brent flickered back into view and stayed visible this time. He was closer than I thought, but turned and ran, amulet clutched in his fist. At this rate, I was afraid we would lose him.

"Trip!" screamed Aunt Nadia with all the magical power she had. In front of us, Brent and seven other people fell over. We would have a lot of explaining to do for that.

Jameson jumped on Brent again and hissed.

Brent didn't move.

What was it about my cat? I could ask later. I had more important things to do now.

I bent down, took the chain of my amulet, and pulled.

Brent didn't let go. "It's mine. I should have inherited it from my mother."

I could feel the amulet's pain more now that I was so close. "You think it would ever do what you wanted? It hates you."

"Once I forced it over my head, it would have no choice, and neither would the cat. The power they have will put me at the head of the fraternity."

Jameson bared his teeth and lunged for Brent's neck.

Instinctively, Brent moved his hands, splaying his fingers to protect himself from Jameson's bite. The amulet fell from his grasp, and I snatched it, pulling the chain over my head in one fast motion.

The screaming in my head stopped, and the dark edges of my vision receded. I fell to the ground next to Brent.

"Get this cat off me," he demanded.

My aunts were starting to help people stand up, now that the trip spell was wearing off.

"Did you feel that? I think it was an earthquake," Aunt Lily said.

What other excuse could there be? No one would believe a tripping spell.

"I didn't think there were any fault lines in New Hampshire," one man in a gray suit said.

"Fracking," Grandma said with authority. "The government's going to ruin the earth right out from under us at this rate."

The man in the suit nodded.

Armed with two different, plausible explanations for why they had fallen, people brushed themselves off and went on their way.

Palmer pulled Brent up and reached for his handcuffs. He had none. He pulled Brent's arm behind his back and put his other hand on Brent's shoulder. "Let's go, big guy."

Together in a tight group, we walked the several blocks to the police station. We were all on the lookout for Brent to attempt another escape, or for the fraternity to try to rescue him. Once they had him, there was no telling what they'd do, though. Maybe he was safer with us.

Palmer marched Brent in through the front door, where Eunice was waiting for us. She raised an eyebrow, but said nothing.

"All of you, stay here. You're needed for questioning, but I need to get him in a cell first."

"Do I need to call my lawyer?" my mother asked.

"Might not be a bad plan. I've got a lot of questions for your family."

He looked at each one of us, waiting for us to agree to stay. When he was satisfied with our nods, he turned and frog-marched Brent back into the depths of the station.

Chapter 28

After a few minutes, the chief came up front. "Lily and Isabella, would you come with me, please?"

I looked to Aunt Lily, and she winked at me. Apparently, everything would be just fine.

We sat in his office, and he closed the door. I seemed to be spending a lot of time here, wondering if I was in trouble or not.

"Ladies, this seems like a delicate situation. How can I help?"

Of all the things he could have said, this was probably the least likely one I could think of. I sat there, thinking, and Aunt Lily took the lead.

"Thank you, Ray. Mr. Thompson has stolen a valuable family heirloom, a necklace, which we have recovered. It was in an evidence bag, and we're concerned the real one might fall into the wrong hands if we give it back."

She took what I thought was the amulet from her purse.

"This is an exact replica, except it doesn't have any... special properties."

His eyes widened. "It's that dangerous?"

"Not dangerous, just powerful."

She handed him the replica. "If we could keep the original, and have this one placed into evidence, that would be best for everyone involved."

He nodded. "Could I see the original?"

I pulled my amulet out from under my shirt. He reached for it but I quickly enclosed it in my fist. "Best not to touch it," I said.

I didn't know anything bad would happen, but I didn't think I could take more screaming and pain from the amulet today.

He looked down at the necklace. "This looks identical. No one will ever know the two have been switched."

He stood up. "I'll be right back."

After the door closed, I asked, "How did you get a replica like that?"

"Once I saw the amulet, it wasn't difficult to put a glamour on an old chain I had laying around. I had a feeling we might need to make a swap."

I had so much to learn about being prepared.

"What is it between you and the chief?"

She smiled, but didn't answer.

The chief returned after a couple minutes.

"Is Mr. Thompson being interrogated?" I asked.

"Not yet. Palmer wants to do the interview himself, but he's furious about Kate, and he's at the hospital with her right now."

"Mr. Thompson's alone?" I asked.

"Don't worry, he's in an interrogation room. There's no way he can escape."

Aunt Lily frowned. "You know he's a ... you know," she said. We never said the word "witch" outside our house.

"For cryin' out loud, Lily! You could have started with that." He rushed out of his office, leaving us alone.

We followed him and were relieved to see through the one-way mirror that Brent was still in the interrogation room. Jameson was sitting, silently, in the back corner of the observation room, focusing all his attention through the mirror and onto Brent.

The chief began to sneeze. "Is there a cat in here?" he asked.

I shook my head, feigning innocence. "I just got a cat, so maybe it's the cat hair on my clothes?"

He sneezed again.

"That's right, chief. There's a cat in there with you," Brent said. "Get rid of the cat, and I'll tell you anything you want to know."

The chief pulled a flashlight out of his utility belt and ran it along the floor.

When the beam reached Jameson, I said, "How did my cat get in here? Come here, boy."

Jameson jumped into my arms and I petted him. "You're such a naughty boy. Cats don't belong in interrogation rooms."

Jameson was not impressed. He flexed his claws and allowed them to barely break my skin. He was going to have something to say about how I was treating him. At least this way, he was able to stay in the room with us.

My amulet glowed faintly, but Jameson blocked the chief from seeing it before I tucked it underneath my shirt. The door to the observation room opened, and Eunice walked in. "Is this the ladies room?" she asked in a surprisingly frail voice.

"No, ma'am. You shouldn't be back here unescorted. Let me find an officer — "

Jameson jumped from my arms and ran back to the corner of the room. "I can help her," I volunteered.

"Thank you, Isabella. That's kind of you."

I smiled. "I'll be right back."

Once I closed the observation room door, Eunice straightened up. "Sorry it took so long to find you. We've got work to do."

She grabbed my hand and the world went gray. "What?" I whispered.

"No one can see us, or hear us, so you don't need to whisper."

She could cast an invisibility spell that could eliminate sound as well? I needed to learn this one.

"Okay. What's the plan?" I asked.

"We need to get into the interrogation room. Tell Jameson to distract the chief."

I didn't understand. "What? You just said no one can hear us."

"Just think about him until you get his attention. Tell him we need a distraction so the chief doesn't see us open the door. The amulet will help you."

I thought about my cat until I could swear I heard his voice in my head. "You don't need to yell. I can hear you."

"Eunice says we need to distract the chief, because we need to get into the interrogation room."

"I'm on it."

I could hear him start to howl at the observation room door.

Eunice opened the door to the interrogation room and dragged me through it with her.

Brent sat up straighter. "I know you're in here," he said.

"Hand on amulet?" Eunice confirmed.

I nodded.

She grabbed my free hand with hers and forced it on Brent's back.

"Hey! Hey, there's someone in here with me," Brent yelled.

"Settle down," the chief said through the intercom. "You're alone."

Brent continued to squirm, but because he was handcuffed to the table, he couldn't move far enough to evade our touch.

"We call on the power of Brigid and command you to accept your punishment."

I felt power from Eunice's hand rush through mine and into Brent's shoulder.

"No!" he cried. "They'll kill me." He looked at the mirror. "Get them out of here!"

The chief and Aunt Lily rushed into the interrogation room. The chief ran to Brent. "Do you need medical attention?"

Aunt Lily held the door open while Eunice and I slipped out. We walked into the now-empty observation room and Eunice let the spell that masked our presence fall away.

"What kind of spell did you use on him?" I asked.

"Congratulations. You just captured your first evil witch. The spell prevents him from escaping police custody again, and from presenting any kind of effective defense in court. He'll be convicted of murder and spend the rest of his life in prison."

One spell would last that long? I was used to spells working for a few minutes, or maybe a few hours before they needed to be recast.

She saw the surprise on my face. "It's the amulets. Their power will sustain the spell."

"Okay, now what do we do?"

"Now I get out of here. You've got some cleaning up to do."

"What do you mean?"

"Your mother said that detective saw a lot more than he should have. You're going to have to wipe his memory—delicately—of the idea that Brent was ever invisible."

I nodded. "With the amulet?"

"Yes."

She opened the door and turned toward the entrance while I turned the other way, to the interrogation room.

I opened the door. "Can I come in?"

Brent took one look at me and said, "Not her. She did this to me. Can't you tell? She's a witch!"

I closed the door, even though I doubted anyone who heard him would think he was telling the truth when he sounded like he was raving.

"Don't be ridiculous. She was taking an old lady to the bathroom. I had my eye on you the entire time. No one was here," the chief said.

Brent sagged in his chair, defeat written on his face.

"I'm going to give you a few minutes to collect yourself, then I'll be back."

The chief turned to us. "Ladies, let's give him a few minutes." He opened the door for us, and followed us out of the interrogation room.

"He won't need a doctor," Aunt Lily said. "He'll calm down in a few minutes." She put her hand on the chief's arm. "Thank you for your help, Ray. My family really appreciates it."

He blushed and said, "My pleasure, Lily. You know I'm here for you whenever you need me."

That was it. I needed to figure out what was going on between the two of them.

Aunt Lily left the chief and me alone.

"What's up between the two of you?" I asked.

He sighed. "If Lily hasn't told you, there's nothing I can say."

Lisa Bouchard

"What did she do to earn your loyalty? You switched evidence for me just because she asked."

"Let's just say she's never steered me wrong, and that when she asks for things, I know they are the right thing to do."

That didn't answer my question, but I could tell I wouldn't get more from him today. "Okay, so what are we going to do with this guy?" I asked.

He laughed. "We?"

"I could talk to him, if you like," I said. "I think I can get him to confess to at least two murders and an attempted home invasion before Palmer gets back."

Chief Dobbins looked at me. I could see indecision on his face; he wasn't sure I could get Brent to confess to anything. I knew as long as he was asking the questions, Brent would have to answer truthfully.

"Wait a minute, two murders?"

"He killed his mother, and probably Agatha Hubert as well. I'd bet dollars to donuts that he was the one who tried to break into my apartment, too."

"And you think you can get him to confess to all that?"

I smiled. "I'm very persuasive when I try."

"Palmer's not going to like this, but you've got fifteen minutes with him. More than that, and people are going to start wondering what's going on."

Chapter 29

Brent recoiled when the chief and I walked into the interrogation room. "I don't want to talk to her. She did something to me."

"Mr. Thompson, you've been read your rights. You are under arrest for reckless driving, but Miss Proctor has more questions for you."

"No way. I'm not talking to her."

"Would you like to call your attorney? I understand you haven't made a call yet."

Brent went pale. "No. No one can know I'm here. I'm not talking to anyone. You don't understand. They'll kill me if I don't bring it to them."

The chief turned to me. "I hate to leave you alone with him. He still doesn't seem very stable."

"He's chained to the table. I'm sure I'll be okay."

I grinned at Brent. "I get it. You don't want to talk witch business. You can talk in front of the chief, though. I've worked with him before, and once we're done, I'll just wipe his mind. Done it plenty of times before, and he doesn't seem to be suffering too many long-term consequences."

"You what?" the chief yelled.

I held my hand out and he stopped talking. He should consider a career in improv, because of course I'd never wiped his memory. I didn't even know how to.

"Now chief, don't worry. There's no sense getting yourself all worked up over something you won't even remember in about an hour's time."

I didn't know if he was playing along with me or if he really thought I'd wiped his memories. I'd have to apologize to him later on.

Brent peered into the chief's eyes. "Are you sure?"

I scoffed. "Easy as pie, once you get the hang of it."

"I don't have to answer your questions."

"Oh, but you have to answer his, don't you?" I asked.

Brent bit his lip.

"Ask him a question, chief, see if he has to answer you."

The chief squared his shoulders. "Who do you think is going to kill you?"

I could feel Brent trying to fight the spell Eunice and I put on him, but he lost. "The fraternity."

"Your fraternity brothers are going to kill you?" the chief asked.

Brent laughed. "The Fraternity of Free Witches."

I leaned back and feigned disinterest. "The fraternity? They can have you for all I care."

"How do you know about us? You just got the amulet."

"You should know better than to think I am alone in anything I do. There's nothing my cat and I can't do."

He blanched at the thought. Jameson really should have told me what a great threat he was.

"But back to the topic at hand. Why shouldn't we let the fraternity have you?"

Brent smirked but didn't answer me. Bats! The spell really only made him accountable to police.

The chief realized he had to re-ask my question. "This is going to get tedious after a while. You need to answer her questions."

Brent furrowed his brow, but then answered. "They'll kill me! After all I've done for them, they'll kill me."

"What exactly have you done for them?" I asked.

"Okay, here's the deal. The fraternity wants all the amulets, across the entire world. If they get enough, they plan to start taking over. You know, like they tried in the 17th century."

No, I didn't know, but there was no way I'd tell him that. I could ask Grandma and Eunice for a history lesson later. "Go on."

"With the amulets, they'd be powerful enough that no one would even dare think the words 'witch trials.' Non-witches would be put to use, serving witches. All we want is to restore the rightful order of the world. Those with power control those without. Just like now, except money will become meaningless, and the ability to cast spells will be everything. We won't hide our power anymore."

My stomach twisted. He sounded like he was talking about the enslavement of most of the world's population.

"You'd enslave millions of people?" I asked, horrified.

"Look around you. Non-magic people are ruining the world. Politics, finances, the environment, war, starvation, any evil you can think of, you can find. Now look at Sewall and the other enclaves around the world. They don't have any of those problems."

"But slavery?" I asked.

He laughed. "We are better, and it's time to start acting like it."

I looked at the chief out of the corner of my eye. He was pale, but remained silent.

"That's never going to happen. You're going to spend the rest of your life in jail," I said.

Now it was Brent's turn to pale. "The fraternity will kill me if they find out where I am. They don't accept failure, and they'll think I talked."

The chief gave Brent his most reassuring smile. "Despite what you might see on tv, it's actually very hard to have someone killed in prison. I'm sure you'll be safe there."

"At least make sure I'm in solitary under a fake name. I'll do anything, waive my right to a trial, just keep me away from them."

"And what's the name of this group again?" the chief asked.

Brent looked at me. "You're going to wipe his memory when we're done?"

I nodded. I seemed to be evading the truth more than a witch who says she doesn't lie ought to.

"The Fraternity of Free Witches."

"And who is in this so-called fraternity?"

"I can only tell you my contact. Caleb Oldman."

"Can't say I'm familiar with that name, but I can make sure he never visits you. Assuming Isabella leaves anything in my memory."

"He wouldn't be dumb enough to come himself. Someone I'd never met would."

"We can't protect you from some vague, faceless, group of people."

Brent leaned forward. "Look, even if I knew anyone other than Caleb, they're recruiting all the time. They could send anyone after me. The faster you get me into solitary under a false name, the safer I'll be."

The chief leaned back and gave Brent a hard stare. "We don't put people in jail without a trial here. You could waive your right to a jury, but that's about all you can do."

This was the moment Brent broke. I could see on his face that he knew he'd die before he saw more than a week in prison. He let his glamour slip and I saw his true face. He had thin burn marks running from his

217

eyes to his chin, and his forehead was raw and blistered, as though he had been held too close to a fire. "Then I'm a dead man."

He turned to me. "Your family can help. You can protect me."

I couldn't believe the nerve he had. He'd killed two people I cared about, and now he thought my family would protect him from the consequences of his actions.

"I could ask Jameson if he'd help, but I doubt he will. I can't do anything until you confess. Start at the beginning."

His shoulders slumped. "The fraternity didn't care what amulet I got for them first, so I tried to get the Lynch amulet. I thought Eunice was weak enough that I could take it from her with no problems, and then maybe I wouldn't have to take my mother's. But Eunice is stronger than I expected, and I couldn't even get close to her. Her wards were so strong, I couldn't get within a half mile of her house. I tried, but I had to give up."

"And when you couldn't get Eunice's?"

"They made me go to my mother. I begged her to just give it to me, but she refused. She said she'd known since I was young that I was too weak to carry it. I was so angry that I decided to show her who was weak and who wasn't."

"What did you do?"

"I went back to her apartment the next night with an aconite tincture and killed my mother because she wouldn't give me the amulet. It was either kill her or the fraternity would do horrible things to me— things that make death look good."

"And Agatha?"

"She heard me talking about the amulet with my fraternity contact. He was pressuring me to get one right away. She found me in Portsmouth, confronted me, and was going to bring me to you. I couldn't let her do that."

"Where did you kill her?"

He allowed himself a small smile. "Right there on the sidewalk in front of The Crispy Biscuit. I put up a cloaking spell, and no one could see that I had her up against the wall, my hand around her throat, squeezing the life out of her."

I shuddered. So it was a cloaking spell that Eunice used to keep anyone from seeing or hearing us in the interrogation room.

"She kept reaching out for people, but no one saw us. I don't think she understood why no one was helping her."

Magic raced across my skin, and before I could control it, a wild spell leaped from my fingers. It's dangerous to be so far out of control, because you never know what spell you'll cast. In this case, I barely managed to avoid hitting him with a small bolt of lightning.

The chief jumped as the energy hit the wall.

"Sorry," I said as we stared at the smoking black mark on the wall barely above Brent's head.

"Why did you teleport her to Eunice's house?" I asked through clenched teeth.

"I thought that if I could get her out of the house, maybe I could figure a way to get in and find her amulet. If I could bring the fraternity two amulets, they might back off me a little. I was desperate, and this looked like my last chance to get at her amulet."

"Anything else you want to confess to?" the chief asked.

"I tried to break into her apartment, but couldn't. I don't suppose that matters much, not compared to two murders."

"No, it doesn't. But at least she won't have to worry about you ever coming back to try again," the chief said.

"Is that all you need from him?" I asked the chief.

"It's plenty. I'll get him processed right away."

"When do you wipe his memory?" Brent asked.

I stood up and walked out with the chief.

I heard Brent scream, "You promised me!" as the interrogation room door closed.

"You don't really erase my memory, do you?" he asked.

"I've never erased yours, or anyone else's memory. I'm not even sure I would know how to do that."

But I'd better figure it out quick, because there was a bit to Palmer's memory he'd be better off without.

I thought I was done at the station, so I said goodbye to the chief and walked out to the reception area. Palmer was there, and he grabbed my arm. "Just the woman I've been looking for."

"How's Kate?" I asked.

He propelled me to his desk and sat me down. "What happened out there?" he asked.

I looked around the open office, full of officers, civilians, and administrative staff. "Is there somewhere we can talk more privately?"

He frowned. "You can't just tell me?"

I shook my head. "I promise, you'd rather it was just between you and me."

He looked unhappy, but said, "Follow me."

I stood up and grabbed my amulet. I called for Jameson, who answered with *You really need to stop yelling. Are you in trouble again?*

I need to erase Palmer's memories of the afternoon. How do I do it?

Jameson chuckled. *That's all? You whisper in his ear everything you want him to forget, then say forget three times.*

That's it?

If you find magic is hard, you're probably doing it wrong. This should work just fine.

Palmer had stopped walking, and I almost ran right into him. "We can talk in here."

"Great."

He opened the door to the conference room and let me go in. I sat down and he sat across the table from me. This was never going to work.

I stood up and sat next to him. "I know this is awkward, but I need to whisper to you."

"No. You don't. This room isn't bugged, and I'm not going to whisper like we're in kindergarten, telling each other secrets."

I whispered "Brent is a witch and used his powers to try and escape. My family caught him because we are also witches."

Of course Palmer didn't hear me.

"What?"

I crooked a finger at him and he leaned toward me. I put one hand on each side of his head and held it still while I repeated my whisper, then said, "Forget, forget, forget."

I released his head and he sat back, shook his head and said, "What were you going to tell me?"

"Just that I need to know if Brent is ever released on bail. He might come after me, or my family, again."

Palmer looked annoyed. "There's already a system in place for that. You'll be notified."

"Thanks. By the way, you never told me how Kate is doing."

"Didn't I? She seems fine. Doctors want to keep her for twenty-four hours, just in case. She was asking for you to visit."

Interesting. I guess she meant it when she said she'd let the past go. "I'll stop by tomorrow."

Chapter 30

I left the station and saw Delia waiting for me. "Hey stranger, want a ride?" she asked.

I didn't even have the option to go to my own apartment. Once I'd been hustled into the kitchen at Proctor House, we all, including Jameson, sat at the table. Six sets of eyes were on me, and I felt like I'd never get out of there until I told them everything.

Before I could begin, Eunice knocked and let herself in. "Did I miss anything?" she asked.

"No. I was just pulling myself together to start explaining everything."

I looked at the seven witches assembled in the kitchen and wondered if I could even tell them everything that had happened over the past few days.

Jameson jumped on my lap and said, "I guess I'll start with a formal introduction. My name is Jameson, and I'm Isabella's new familiar. It's difficult for me to talk to people I'm not bonded to, so she's going to have to tell most of the story, and I'll let you know when she gets it wrong."

"What do you mean, when I get it wrong?" I asked.

He looked up at me. "Humans always get something wrong."

I wished I could tell him he was mistaken.

Aunt Nadia stood up and started looking through the cabinets. She pulled out a can of tuna and put it in one of our special Wedgewood bowls. Wedgewood! For a cat? "I apologize that we don't have any fresh for you, but we will the next time you visit."

Jameson jumped down off my lap and rubbed against Aunt Nadia's leg before beginning to eat the tuna.

"Okay, I'll start at the beginning. There's a lot we didn't learn about being witches."

"What do you mean?" Delia asked.

"For instance, there are some witches who are responsible for keeping others safe. Apparently, I'm one of them now."

"Is that why you have a familiar?" Thea asked.

I nodded. "Jameson is going to teach me everything I need to know about the Sorority of Brigid, protecting witches, and keeping our sanctuary towns thriving."

"Safe from who?" my mother asked.

"There's this group, the Fraternity of Free Witches, who think the world would be better if they were in charge. Mrs. Thompson's son was one of them, and it was his job to steal this."

I pulled out my amulet, and it glowed because it was close to Eunice's.

"He originally wanted to steal Eunice's, but he couldn't get close to her house, so he had to try to get his mother's."

"I thought these were passed down in families," Aunt Lily said.

"Usually they are, but Mrs. T. knew she couldn't give it to her son."

Jameson jumped on the kitchen table. "She left Sewall just before he was about to take it from her. She left so fast, she couldn't bring anything with her except me. She was drawn to Portsmouth and hoped she'd find a witch here that she could trust."

"That's why she had so little in her apartment," Delia said.

"Brent wanted to take the amulet, but she wouldn't give it to him. Finally, the fraternity pressured him so much, and from what I saw when his glamour slipped, tortured him enough, that he killed his mother," I said.

"But he still couldn't find the amulet?" Aunt Lily asked.

"No. That's why he was so interested in Jameson. He thought maybe he could find it if he had the familiar."

"But that's backward. If he had taken me, I would have just been a cat to him. I would never choose someone like him to be my human."

"I don't understand this sorority thing," my mother said. "It sounds like another job."

I looked to Eunice. "I don't know much about it, but I think Eunice and Jameson will teach me."

Eunice cleared her throat. "We'll get her up to speed quickly. Faith can help, too."

"And is she in any danger right now?" Grandma asked.

"No. Not now. The fraternity will take some time to regroup after losing Brent. We'll try to keep her inheritance of the amulet a secret for as long as possible," Eunice said.

I wanted to keep talking, but I was exhausted. After my third yawn, Thea took pity on me. "Maybe we can continue this tomorrow?"

"Can you drive me home?" I asked, feeling too tired to walk.

She nodded and we left before anyone could object.

"You're a pretty big deal now, aren't you?" Thea asked as she pulled her car out of the driveway.

I ran my hand down Jameson's back. He'd fallen asleep as soon as he'd finished the bowl of tuna. "I don't feel like it. I feel like an exhausted witch with too much responsibility and not enough information to know what to do."

"You know you can count on me and Delia, right? Just like always?"

I smiled in the darkness. "Thanks."

When I got out of the car, she said, "Call if you need anything."

Jameson woke up and walked in with me. I unlocked my apartment door and turned the alarm off.

0904. What had started as a nice reminder of our friendship stung now that Abby wasn't here.

I sat on the couch and Jameson jumped up beside me. "So, I don't really know how our relationship is supposed to work."

"It's best if you just do what I say and feed me plenty of salmon."

"Salmon's not cheap. How do you plan to earn your keep around here?"

"You'll work it out."

"But honestly, how do I treat you? What happens when Abby moves back in and I want to talk to you?"

"Abby will never be able to hear me, but I don't think she'll move back in, either. She's too afraid."

"How about Palmer? Or Kate?"

Jameson shook his head. "Only witches, and even then, not all of them. It's too exhausting."

"Are you really two hundred years old, or are you just two hundred cat years?"

"Cat years?"

"Yeah, you know. Like every human year is seven dog years."

"I was born in 1811, and I look remarkably good for my age."

I scratched between his ears. "Yes, you do. Are you really a cat? Or are you something else masquerading as a cat?"

"I'm an enchanted cat." He yawned. "I've had a busy day and I've missed at least two of my naps. Can we save the twenty questions for another time?"

"Oh, sorry. Yes. Do you mind if I make some popcorn and watch a movie?"

He jumped off the couch and walked into Abby's room. "As long as I can't hear it from *my* room, I don't care what you do."

I rolled my eyes. This was going to be an interesting relationship.

I'd just finished making popcorn and turning on my tv when there was a knock at my door. It was Palmer. I knew before I even got up. Was I beginning to recognize his knock, or was the amulet starting to tell me things? I wasn't sure.

"Come on in. Any updates on Kate?"

"She's fine. They're letting her go tomorrow afternoon, but so far, no one knows why she fainted like she did."

"Is that what happened?"

"Looks like it. Unless you know anything different."

I shook my head. "No clue. Want some popcorn? I was just about to start a movie. Want to stay?"

He rubbed his temples. "This isn't a social call. How did you get Thompson to confess to both murders?"

"Maybe you should sit down. You look stressed."

He sat on the couch. "Of course I'm stressed. A woman I'd never heard of three months ago suddenly pops into my life and has solved three murders and a kidnapping case."

"Don't forget, one attempted home invasion as well."

He scowled. "You're not helping yourself here."

I beamed at him and held the popcorn bowl out. He looked suspicious and didn't take any.

"Oh, for crying out loud," I said. I took a big handful and ate it. "There. It's safe for you to eat."

"Maybe I'll use a bit more manners, though." He took a couple kernels and ate them.

"Sea salt?" he asked.

"And garlic butter."

"It's good. Now tell me how you're doing my job better than I am."

I wanted so much to taunt him and say that maybe he wasn't so good at his job, but that wouldn't be fair. He was a good detective; he just didn't have the same skill set I had. And with the amulet and Jameson, I was afraid I'd only become a better detective over time.

I shrugged. "Beginner's luck?"

"I doubt that. There's something about you. Something about your whole family that has my radar pinging in every direction. You're not normal women, but I can't put my finger on why I think that."

"Maybe it's because there are no men in the family?"

He shook his head. "Too easy. It's something deeper."

He had good instincts. Maybe someday he'd figure it out.

"Get your bag, it's time to head out."

"What? I'm exhausted. I don't want to go anywhere."

"Don't think it escaped my notice that you were driving a car earlier today. I let it slide, because there were much bigger issues to deal with, but I can't have you breaking the law like that."

I looked up at him. He didn't sound angry, even when he ought to. "What are we going to do?"

"I've got a buddy at the DMV. I'm giving you the time it takes to drive there to prove to me you should have a license. If you pass, he'll give you one."

"Oh. Ah, I haven't studied for the test. I'm not ready."

"Don't make me spell out the ways I'm bending the law for you. Let's go."

Outside, his Highlander was waiting in the parking lot. "You want me to drive? Really?"

He tossed me the keys. "Get in. Don't forget to check your mirrors."

I unlocked the doors and climbed in. I had to adjust the seat and mirrors. "You serious? You're not going to arrest me for driving without a license?"

He shook his head. "Just pay attention, don't get into an accident, and turn left out of the parking lot."

I started the car and silently called on Brigid for help. I wasn't sure if that was how her protection worked, but it couldn't hurt.

We drove to the DMV without incident, so upon reflection, Brigid seemed to protect me when I called. I even parallel parked his large car correctly.

"Good. Now we get your picture taken and you get a license."

This was definitely not how getting a driver's license worked. "Don't I need to bring in a bunch of ID and proof of insurance and stuff like that?"

"You've got a non-driving ID, and I put you on my insurance. You'll get your own insurance right away, but for now, you're on mine."

Why would he go out of his way for me like this and put me on his insurance? "I don't understand, and I feel uncomfortable knowing you've done me such a large favor."

"Tomorrow I have to finish the paperwork on the Thompson case, and seeing you driving without a license has to be part of it. This way, when your name is run, they'll see you have a license, and I must have been mistaken."

"But why?"

"I can't arrest Kate's friend. Not when Kate's in the hospital."

"So you're making it look like I wasn't breaking the law by breaking the law yourself?"

He groaned in exasperation. "Maybe you don't have to overanalyze this. Maybe you can just take the favor, say thank you, and try to stay out of trouble from now on."

I grinned. "I guess I could do that."

The door to the DMV opened, and a man who must have been Palmer's buddy came out. "Didn't look like the two of you were going to stop arguing, so I used the picture on her ID."

He handed me a laminated paper driver's license.

"Two days retroactive." He looked at Palmer. "We're even now?"

"Yeah, we're even."

"Good. I've gotta get home."

I turned back to Palmer. "Now what?"

"Now I take you home and get back to my paperwork."

His stomach growled.

"How about I make you dinner first? It only seems fair," I said.

"You can cook?" he asked.

"Absolutely. I used to work at a bakery." Dinners, though, were much trickier. "I make a mean grilled cheese and tomato soup."

"I'll take it."

The End

Excerpt of Romaine Calm

Isabella Proctor Mysteries
Book Three

Chapter One

Usually, people train their pets, not the other way around.

I pulled the heavy wooden door to the Portsmouth Apothecary closed. The doorbells chimed as I locked up my business. I rested a hand on one of the cool glass panes and quickly refreshed the protection wards. Done with my evening ritual, I took a deep breath of late fall air and headed for home because I had a date.

Okay, not a date. An appointment. With my cat.

Before I start to sound too much like a crazy cat lady, let me explain.

Jameson, the cat in question, was my familiar and he was taking his responsibility to train me seriously. About a month ago, I was given a beautiful emerald amulet by my neighbor. Jameson, my cat, came with the amulet, along with some serious responsibilities. When I accepted the amulet, I became the newest member of the Sorority of Brigid. The sorority was a group of witches whose goals were to keep witchcraft - real witchcraft, not the stuff you see on TV - a secret, keep witches safe, and prevent witches from abusing their power.

To hear Jameson tell it, the sorority should be all I thought about and my foolish notions about having to pay my rent or buy food shouldn't concern me.

Yeah, well, I really enjoyed having a roof over my head and when I threatened to toss him outside during a rainstorm he decided I might have a point after all.

At any rate, I was on my way home for more training. Begrudgingly, he said I was okay with a lot of the larger and simpler spells, so we were working on precision with smaller spells. When I asked about the focus I'd chosen in my last investiture, potions, he laughed.

"Everything changes once you join the sorority," he said.

"What changed for you?" I asked.

"I'm not a member."

"Oh," I said, feeling stupid. "Is it a humans-only group?"

"No. It's for witches and their familiars. But when I was a kitten, the sorority and fraternity were split along traditional lines. The Sorority of Brigid was strictly for women and the Fraternity of Free Witches only allowed men."

"Then why aren't you the familiar for someone in the fraternity?"

"Because I'm not evil."

The jury was out on that. Some of the spells he had me casting were so difficult I felt like my brain would explode.

I went to my family with some of my concerns, but they were no help. I wasn't sure any of them ever had a familiar.

Aunt Lily said I needed to follow his training. She was certain he knew what was best. He was, after all, over two hundred years old and had trained at least three other witches before me.

Aunt Nadia thought I could get to him through his stomach. You know - the best way to a man's heart and all that. Maybe that applied to cats, too.

My mother didn't know what I ought to do. She had a more realistic view of my relationship with Jameson, because she heard more of my complaints than my aunts. She'd started coming to visit me once a week at the apothecary. She never brought up the previously sore subject of me moving home, so the visits were relaxing. If I'd known all it took for her to stop haranguing me about moving home was to get a familiar, I'd have gone looking for one a long time ago.

She thought I was stuck with Jameson, unless I wanted to give up the amulet.

I'd considered the idea, but I didn't want to miss out on the power it gave me, and the ability to help people in addition to my work at the apothecary. I didn't think the amulet liked the idea of being passed on to someone else, either.

Over the past month I thought we were becoming more in tune. I strode down the sidewalk on my way home for a quick dinner and night of training. We'd been working on my fine control, so he had me do the most excruciatingly difficult things, like move just one piece of ice in a glass while holding all the others still. Or making just one of the fronds on my palm tree move.

I could see where witches preferred to train in areas they're naturally good at. I was okay at spellwork, but the level he had me working at was exhausting.

At least I slept well at night.

I walked into my apartment. "I'm home," I called out.

Jameson was waiting for me, sitting on the kitchen counter. I'd tried to instill the idea that cats don't sit on the food preparation or eating surfaces, but he didn't care.

"Good. I'm hungry and you've got a lot of training to do tonight."

I rolled my eyes. "Same thing we do every night, Pinky."

He cocked his head, clearly not understanding my '90s cartoon reference. I thought he'd get it because at least he was alive then. I was a long way from being able to take over the world. And even if I did, what would I do with it?

"Start by opening the can of salmon cat food without using your hands.

I frowned at him. "No dinner for me first?"

"I thought it would be nice for us to eat together," he said.

"Right. Okay then." I considered the cans of Purina Pro Plan he preferred. They had a ring pull to open them, but when he said no hands, he meant no hands at all - no holding the can in one hand and using a fork handle to pop the top open.

Another thing he insisted on was subtle magic. It was no good trying to keep magic a secret if I was obvious every time I tried to use it. He had a point there, but I wished I could start off with big gestures and then move into smaller ones. Big gestures made the magic easier to use, at least for me.

I pointed my index finger flicked it from right to left to open the cat food cabinet. One more gesture had the can floating down to the counter. I considered how to open it without my hands. There were a couple ways I could do it, but which was best? I could force the can to stay on the counter as I levitated a fork and used the handle to open it. I could try the metal shearing spell to cut the top of the can off, or I could try to make the can explode and hope I was fast enough to catch the food and direct it into the bowl.

Lisa Bouchard

I wasn't feeling up to cleaning cat food off the walls if I didn't catch the exploding food, and using a fork didn't seem very impressive, so I went for the metal shearing spell.

I started the can slowly spinning, then focused my mind on creating a sharp point, just above the inside edge of the can. I lowered the point and thin curls of metal started peeling away from the lid. It was working! I pushed the point down and felt more resistance. I increased the can's rotation speed and within two seconds, the top of the can was cut off.

At this point, he would let me take the lid off and dump the food into his bowl, but I was so pleased with myself that I decided to show off. I levitated the lid to the recycling, then slowly lowered the can to his empty bowl. I upended it, gave the bottom a sharp magical tap, and smiled as the food fell out into his bowl. Success!

The can levitated to the sink to be rinsed and I was done.

I beamed at my cat.

"Moderately acceptable. Now, what are you going to eat?"

"Moderately acceptable? Are you kidding me! Did you see what I did there? I held the can down, and made it spin, and used a sharp blade of air - of air! - to cut the lid off. I did great."

Jameson was a master of using his tone to get his feelings across. "I can only hope that your standards will raise as you get better at spellcasting. For now, I'll say you were well within the bounds of acceptable."

I turned my back on my familiar and opened the fridge. My spells usually rated 'marginally acceptable' or 'I suppose that will work, too' so I should probably take his words as a compliment.

I'd had teachers who were in the school of 'don't praise students until they are perfect' and although I didn't thrive that way, I could work with it.

My fridge was mostly empty. I worked a lot and ate dinner at Proctor House at least one night a week, where Aunt Nadia forced leftovers on me. She loved me and this was one of the ways she showed it. Maybe tomorrow night I'd head over and see what they were having.

But for tonight, it was frozen pizza.

Chapter 2

I opened the heavy glass door to the Crispy Biscuit and scanned the mostly occupied tables, searching for my friend Mina. The Biscuit was busy for a Tuesday morning and it took a minute for me to look through all the tables I could see from the door.

I hadn't seen Mina since she left for college a year before I graduated from high school. I didn't have many friends then, and I hardly had time to make new ones now, so I took care to keep the ones I had.

"Isabella, over here!" I heard her call.

I turned to her voice and saw her waving her arms to get my attention. She was wearing a fuchsia tank top that contrasted with her long, lime green hair. How had I not seen her immediately?

over corrected and was about to fall into us. Without thinking, I wiggled a finger and made the air behind her solid. She bumped into the air but was then able to right herself, only spilling a bit of juice on her tray. She turned around and held her hand out, looking for whatever solid thing she'd bumped into, but I'd already released the spell.

"That was close," Mina said.

"What was?"

"That waitress, she almost fell with a tray full of drinks."

"Oh, I wasn't paying attention," I lied. What? It's not like she'd believe me if I told her what really happened.

Emma delivered her drinks and came to take our order. "Mina! It's been so long since I've seen you. How are you?"

"Really great, thanks."

From the kitchen, we heard the cook calling Emma to retrieve an order. "Sorry I can't chat. Can I take your order?"

I didn't have to look at the menu. "Can I get an omelet with spinach, onion, mushroom and swiss, with rye toast and a mug of coffee?"

"Of course. And you, Mina?"

"Waffles with strawberries and whipped cream, and a glass of orange juice."

Emma gave us a quick smile then rushed to the kitchen to pick up her order.

Behind me, I heard the crash of plates falling to the floor. I turned around and saw a man in distress, banging the table. Detective Palmer, who was on the other side of the booth, jumped up and pulled the man to the floor.

Palmer frantically patted down the wheezing man's pockets. Within seconds, the man's wheezing grew softer and then stopped. His chest stopped moving up and down, too.

Palmer looked at the crowd and saw me. "Isabella, call 911."

I grabbed my phone and dialed. "I'm calling for Detective Steve Palmer. There's a man in respiratory distress and," I looked back over at him, "he looks like he's going into anaphylaxis."

"Does anyone have an epi pen?" Palmer shouted.

Emma ran into the kitchen and then fought her way through the crowd of onlookers to bring him the restaurant's emergency pen.

Palmer jammed the orange end of the Epipen on the now motionless man's leg.

"We're sending help to your location," the operator said to me.

"He's not moving now, and I don't think he's breathing."

With the phone to my ear, I turned to Mina. "Go wait outside for the ambulance and make sure they can get in."

She nodded and walked off to the door.

Palmer was on his knees, doing chest compressions, and crying. I'd never seen him display much emotion, unless it was anger in an interrogation room and I felt for him.

Now that it appeared there may be a dead body on the floor of the restaurant, people were quickly paying and leaving. I swiped some napkins from a nearby table, went to Palmer and sat next to him, my leg touching his so that he knew he wasn't alone.

I sat with him, silently, until Mina led the EMTs to us. Palmer never stopped trying to save the man's life.

As soon as he saw their uniforms, something snapped back into place in Palmer's mind. He stood up, surrendered the epipen, and began to answer questions efficiently. The paramedic who was taking care of the patient looked to his partner and shook his head.

Palmer went pale and I steadied him. "Take it easy there, big guy." I moved him to a seat and gently pressed his shoulder until he sat.

Chief Dobbins strode in. He looked at the paramedics, who shook their heads. "Thanks, you two can go," he said.

He called for a coroner on his radio.

I squeezed Palmer's shoulder and said, "I'm going to leave you with the chief." To the chief I said, "Please call if I can help."

I met Mina back at our table. I sat, exhausted. Our food hadn't arrived, but I was too upset to eat. "I can't eat anything. I'm going to head to the apothecary."

She stood up. "Me either. I paid for breakfast, you can leave the tip."

I put a ten on the table and we walked out.

"Friend of yours?" Mina asked.

Was he? "It's complicated. He's a police detective, and I've worked with him a few times. I've never seen him cry, though. I wonder who the other guy was?"

Romaine Calm is available for preorder now!

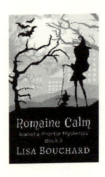

Looking for more by Lisa Bouchard?

Join my mailing list at
LisaBouchard.com for a free prequel
novella!

Other Books by Lisa Bouchard

About the Author

It all started when she learned to read at five. One of her first and favorite memories is of words taped to all the objects in the house. Not long after that, books became the best thing ever and there was no turning back.

She suffered a crisis of confidence in High School and College and decided writing was too difficult, so she earned a degree in Chemistry and later enrolled in a Physics PhD program instead. Three career changes and four children later, she's back to writing and much happier for it.

Now she works from her home office in New Hampshire amid the books, kids, and occasional pets. Visit her at http://LisaBouchard.com.

Made in the USA
Middletown, DE
13 June 2022

Mina had never been a shrinking violet and as she stood up and met me in the aisle to pull me into a tight hug, I knew nothing had changed.

"I've missed you so much," she yelled in my ear.

I squeezed her back and broke the hug before she had the chance to do lasting damage to my hearing.

She grabbed my hand and dragged me to our booth. I sat across from her and stared at her for a moment. She had a worried look but it broke when she smiled. "You look amazing. Tell me everything."

"Well, I inherited a business and it's taking everything I've got to run it. It's exhausting."

"Really? What kind of business?"

"It's an apothecary. I spent about a year as an apprentice before it became mine." I stopped talking as thoughts of finding Trina's murdered body flooded my mind.

Mina touched my hand. "Hey, are you okay?"

I looked back up at her. "Yeah, sorry. It's just that I inherited the apothecary after my mentor was murdered."

She frowned. "That's horrible. I'm so sorry to hear that."

Instinctively, my hand went to the amulet I hadn't taken off since I was inducted into the Society of Brigid. The amulet, and the approval of my familiar, granted me admission to the Society of Brigid, the group of witches tasked with keeping all witches safe, secret, and from using their power for evil.

"Oh, nice necklace," Mina said.

I'd gotten tired of explaining that the good things that had come to me lately were because someone had died. The apothecary, the amulet, and my black cat Jameson. It was starting to feel ghoulish. "Thanks. It was a gift from a friend. Enough about me. How about you? What was your major again?"

Mina laughed. "Equine therapy."

I furrowed my brow. "Like being a physical therapist for animals?"

She straightened the sugar packets in their small container. "No, like using horses to help people's mental and physical health."

"That sounds like you - always helping other people. And fun if you like nature and being outdoors all the time." Mina had never been big on the outdoors but people could change.

"I do. Horses are majestic animals and they seem to know the patients are vulnerable and act accordingly." She took a sip of water and continued. "Unfortunately, there are no facilities hiring in a five hundred mile radius."

"Five hundred?" I asked.

"Yeah. I've sent my resume to each of them, then did follow up calls when no one got back to me."

"Wow. You'd think at least one of them would have called back."

She gave me a wry smile. "Yeah, you'd think."

"So what are you going to do now?" I asked.

She was about to answer me when Emma, who was walking past us, yelped. Emma was in the process of a slow-motion fall. She tried to regain her balance but over corrected and was about to fall into us. Without thinking, I wiggled a finger and made the air behind her solid. She bumped into the air but was then able to right herself, only spilling a bit of juice on her tray. She turned around and held her hand out, looking for whatever solid thing she'd bumped into, but I'd already released the spell.

"That was close," Mina said.

"What was?"

"That waitress, she almost fell with a tray full of drinks."

"Oh, I wasn't paying attention," I lied. What? It's not like she'd believe me if I told her what really happened.

Emma delivered her drinks and came to take our order. "Mina! It's been so long since I've seen you. How are you?"

"Really great, thanks."

From the kitchen, we heard the cook calling Emma to retrieve an order. "Sorry I can't chat. Can I take your order?"

I didn't have to look at the menu. "Can I get an omelet with spinach, onion, mushroom and swiss, with rye toast and a mug of coffee?"

"Of course. And you, Mina?"

"Waffles with strawberries and whipped cream, and a glass of orange juice."

Emma gave us a quick smile then rushed to the kitchen to pick up her order.

Behind me, I heard the crash of plates falling to the floor. I turned around and saw a man in distress, banging the table. Detective Palmer, who was on the other side of the booth, jumped up and pulled the man to the floor.

Palmer frantically patted down the wheezing man's pockets. Within seconds, the man's wheezing grew softer and then stopped. His chest stopped moving up and down, too.

Palmer looked at the crowd and saw me. "Isabella, call 911."

I grabbed my phone and dialed. "I'm calling for Detective Steve Palmer. There's a man in respiratory distress and," I looked back over at him, "he looks like he's going into anaphylaxis."

"Does anyone have an epi pen?" Palmer shouted.

Emma ran into the kitchen and then fought her way through the crowd of onlookers to bring him the restaurant's emergency pen.

Palmer jammed the orange end of the Epipen on the now motionless man's leg.

"We're sending help to your location," the operator said to me.

"He's not moving now, and I don't think he's breathing."

With the phone to my ear, I turned to Mina. "Go wait outside for the ambulance and make sure they can get in."

She nodded and walked off to the door.

Palmer was on his knees, doing chest compressions, and crying. I'd never seen him display much emotion, unless it was anger in an interrogation room and I felt for him.